-THE-
ANT
HEAP

THE ANT HEAP

a novel by

Margit Kaffka

Adapted into English from the Hungarian and introduced by

Charlotte Franklin

Marion Boyars
London • New York

Published in Great Britain and the United States
in 1995 by Marion Boyars Publishers
24 Lacy Road, London, SW15 1NL
237 East 39th Street, New York, NY 10016

Distributed in Australia by Peribo Pty Ltd
58 Beaumont Road, Mount Kuring-gai, NSW 2080

Originally published in Hungary in 1917 by Nyugat under the title
Hangyaboly

British Library Cataloguing in Pulication Data
Kaffka, Margit
Ant Heap
I. Title II. Franklin, Charlotte
894.51133 [F]

Library of Congress Cataloging in Publication Data
Kaffka, Margit.
[Hangyaboly. English]
The Ant Heap / Margit Kaffka; adapted into English from the Hungarian by Charlotte Franklin; with an introduction by Charlotte Franklin.
I. Franklin, Charlotte. II. Title.
PH3281.K22H313 1995
894'.51133--dc20 94-12706

ISBN 0–7145–2989–3 Original Paperback

Typeset in 11/13pt Palm Springs and Prose Antique by
Ann Buchan (Typesetters), Shepperton
Printed on acid-free paper by
Biddles Ltd, Guildford and King's Lynn

For my parents Éva and Kálmán Hajnal-Kónyi

who enjoyed their Shakespeare in Hungarian
as well as in English

MARGIT KAFFKA

A chance trail led me to Margit Kaffka via her friend and rival Anna Lesznai (1885–1966), whose exuberantly busy water colour of a peasant pilgrimage and crowded colourful embroidery of a pear tree had found their way into my possession. Both these works were beautiful, and I wanted to know more about the artist. Her surname, that of a Slovak village, proved to be the *nom de plume* of Amalia Moscowitz, a friend of my grandparents. I enjoyed reading her poems and autobiographical novel. With my husband I went in search of her to Hungary, to the museum of her works in Hatvan, sixty kilometres east of Budapest, and was impressed by the scope of her talent. We continued into Romania — Transylvania, part of the old Hungary — which seemed like the back of beyond, a return to former times. Geese, naked from the plucking of their downy feathers, roamed beneath unpruned pear trees, no cars were on the roads, hardly a bicycle. We visited the house of Anna Lesznai's second husband, Oszkár Jászi, distinguished liberal of his day, advocate of rights for ethnic minorities; next door was a plaque commemorating the Hungarian writer Margit Kaffka — a rare honour from present day Romania.

The lives of these two outstanding women were intertwined in many ways. They were mutually fascinated by their differences of class, religious background, education and, especially, temperament. Amusingly, each wrote about the other in her fiction — while also revealing herself. Margit Kaffka wrote a brilliant contemporary novel chronicling and contrasting their experience, against the glamorous background of Budapest. Anna Lesznai wrote her version with hindsight forty years on and from New York.

Kaffka had to struggle against prejudice: for education, independence from her family, for a literary career. Lesznai, of a wealthy Jewish family, was a lonely little rich girl — but encouraged by her milieu into artistic endeavour. Both women had admired their fathers, put them on pedestals, produced poems in their memory — but felt more critical of their mothers' passivity. One family had risen rapidly in the world, the other declined. Lesznai's grandfather, Moscowitz, had bought a splendid estate at about the time Margit's family on her mother's side had to sell theirs. Margit Kaffka knew she would have to earn her own living, an activity despised by her family, particularly for a woman! 'Both came', Lesznai wrote in her novel, 'as innocent souls to the corrupt city of Budapest.' Both of them adored the stimulation they found there. Both of them were young divorced mothers. Anna Lesznai with peasant wet nurses for her babies was not too worried. She could send the children to her mother to be looked after. She wrote, and beautifully illustrated, stories for her sons — and was deeply concerned when they became ill. This is now called 'quality time' mothering. As any middle-class woman in Budapest, Margit Kaffka had a servant girl to help her, but from bitter knowledge she wrote about the stress of conflicting loyalties for a working mother worrying about her child.

In sexual behaviour Lesznai had no notion of different standards for men and women — she divorced two husbands who did not share this point of view; the wondrous joy of sexual fulfilment continued into old age. She felt no envy for the male world; her only brother and eldest son were killed in wars. In spite of a theoretical acceptance of sexual emancipation, Margit Kaffka was conscious of the customs of discipline. There were complications with every love affair.

The admired Hungarian poet of the period, Endre Ady, praised their poems. Kaffka, five years older than Lesznai, had reviewed generously a volume of her verse, recognizing a kindred spirit: 'a modern woman's voice, not defeated by motherhood, or accepting subservience, rather, expecting fulfilment as of right.' And Lesznai yielded the literary crown to Margit: 'She was the only woman regarded by men as a writer of equal status, a surprising person, combining qualities of beauty and plainness in rare harmony. She bore her extraordinary talent as an unwelcome gift.'

Hungarian friends urged me to read and understand Margit Kaffka. I loved the strength of her prose: vivid, honest, refreshing. The poetry for which she is also admired was difficult for me. Surprising myself, I resolved on an entirely new, presumptuous and absorbing project — to translate her last novel, the story of six months in the life of a convent entitled *Hangyaboly* (*The Ant Heap*). This novel seemed an excellent introduction to the writing of Margit Kaffka; lightly but firmly her own philosophy shines through the book. The unexpected metaphor in the title evokes the busy life of a convent which buzzes angrily when disturbed by the outside world. Her gift of sharp observation surprised her readers, and distressed those who recognized themselves in what she wrote. Her own view survives in a letter: 'The author is like an ostrich burying its head in the sand. . . . Writing is a ruthless profession demanding blood sacrifice.' She was merciless to her own class, holding the mirror to a corrupt society of gentry clinging to feudal ways. The Order of the Sisters of Mercy, which trained Margit Kaffka, never forgave her for writing *The Ant Heap*.

She was born on June 10th, 1880 in the provincial town of Nagykároly (now Carei in Romania). She believed her restless temperament was the result of mixed ancestry, between a Hungarian mother and Slav father, Gyula Kaffka, who died at the age of thirty-four when Margit was only six years old; his death ended her happy childhood. The young family was left destitute; grandparents made themselves responsible for his youngest daughter, not for Margit the eldest. Her mother — brought up in high provincial society, to catch men at dances, with few other skills beyond running a household and entertaining in the proper manner — felt bound to marry again; but her second husband turned out to be unsatisfactory financially and in other ways. Observant and sensitive, young Margit squirrelled away these memories and years later wrote her best selling novel *Szinek és Évek (Colours and Years)* about her mother's hopeless predicament. The widow as the object of unkind local tittle-tattle also appears in *The Ant Heap*.

Margit Kaffka was a misfit in her stepfather's household. She was sent to board in a local convent, rather like those schools where the Brontë sisters were educated in Yorkshire at the beginning of the nineteenth century — a horrifying experience. One of Margit's earliest short stories, 'Letters from the Convent', is the moving account of a little girl who suffers from neglect and lack of affection, harsh punishment, the cold, the damp, bad food, but is always writing hopeful letters to no avail: there is a new stepfather and she dies! Today this may read sentimentally, but it was inspired by her own experience.

Margit remained in the convent for three years. In an autobiographical short story, 'Triumph', she described her feelings on re-entering normal life: 'I was ten and had only recently returned in bad health from a distant convent school where I had spent three years; three years, stunted, day dreaming with sick fantasies, physically weak. There I could never see bright sunshine, flowers in the meadows or even a living dog. I must have been quite different from other children.'

After this she attended the local secondary school boarding with relatives. Her grades in school reports have been published in Hungary; she was a good pupil, took part in performances, and wrote for the student journal.

Her town, Nagykároly, was peaceful, remote, dominated by its feudal castle, but with an emerging middle class. Margit's family felt socially superior to such upstarts; she herself felt attracted by new liberal ideas and admired 'western' thought. Nagykároly had its share of other nationalities: German settlers, Romanians, Jews, Gypsies, Italians and Slovaks all appear in her novels. She loved Nagykároly, its gardens, seasons, the countryside, but found unbearable the gossip and small-town mentality of its inhabitants. Determined not to follow her mother's example in trusting herself entirely to marriage, Margit went back to her convent to gain a diploma for teaching in primary schools. In return for board and training she had to promise one more year of work as a teacher at a school run by the Sisters of Mercy. In *The Ant Heap* mention is made of such an arrangement — the poor girls get caught out by the nuns for their cynicism. Kaffka was able to transfer for this last year to the town of Miskolc (nearer Budapest but very provincial) where her paternal grandparents lived.

At the end of it all, free and qualified to teach in the State system, the next job on offer was still in a convent! To her cousin she wrote: 'To sweat it out again in a convent — when my whole soul is drawn to the secular schools for new active work. The Church has become out-dated with such strict prejudiced institutions. The spirit is different there, according to the Reverend Mother proposing this job, and I dared not contradict — since it's the spirit which has persecuted and embittered me these four long years.' Luckily, her mother was able to use some influence and Margit achieved her desire to go to Budapest in 1899. On a scholarship she spent the next three years at the prestigious Erzsébet Training College for Women studying for her Higher Diploma, and became a qualified Secondary School Teacher in 1902. Her experiences there are captured in her novel *Mária Évei (The Years of Mary).*

During this time her poetry and short stories began to be published and noticed. Margit's mother had sent some of her early poems to a literary member of the family. The answer she received is often quoted: 'Dear cousin, Your daughter's poems are not bad, indeed rather beautiful and quite good. But why should a woman write? For such an excellent housewife as yourself it would be a great pity if your daughter were to forsake the culinary arts. In fact it is a waste of time for her to become a teacher!' (In Hungary, *far* more than in England, the art of cooking was considered the essential accomplishment for a woman, to conquer and then keep her man. The kitchen was the woman's space. A friend wrote of Margit: 'she wielded her pen as our mothers did their mixing spoons.')

In 1905 Margit, feeling she was getting on in years, agreed to marry a handsome forestry engineer, Bruno Fröhlich. Margit hated life in the provincial town far away from metropolitan culture, housekeeping was not her forte, she felt suffocated by domesticity; and she continued to write and also to teach for financial reasons. She gave birth in 1906 to her only child, a son László. Motherhood was a turning point in her understanding of women. Poets writing honestly about motherhood are rare; though not in fact written for her own son, 'Petike Jár' ('Peter's First Steps') is a favourite in Hungarian anthologies, the delightful observation of a toddler's first steps, stumbling and determined to reach his mother, encouraging himself by echoing her words, 'careful! careful!', without fully understanding them. The last stanza looks ahead to the time when Peter, an energetic young man, will visit his mother who, still anxious, hobbles out to greet him.

Her first marriage had not been a success and by 1910 she had separated from her husband, resuming her maiden name as a writer; she lived in Budapest as a single mother supporting herself by teaching and writing stories, reviews, educational books for children. Ambitious to be good in all her roles as writer, teacher, mother, housewife, she was constantly rushing between home and her job at the school. Margit was lonely, sometimes suicidal; creativity was therapy. She wrote poems but found her true voice in prose.

In spite of social criticism, she sat down with the men in smoky coffee-houses and became part of the small circle of modern writers who were dedicated to new writing. Their journal was called *Nyugat* (*The*

West). It appeared twice a month. It was brilliantly edited by a poet with the pseudonym, Ignotus, a name still worn proudly by his descendants. Sari Ignotus, the daughter of that editor, now aged ninety-one and living in London remembers Margit Kaffka: 'She was the only one of those writers coming to my father's house who knew how to talk to a child. She was a marvellous woman.' In Budapest there is a delightful museum honouring these revered writers of a golden age. Evocative photographs and colourful typography can convey the spirit of the times even to a non-Hungarian reader. It meant much to Margit to be included in this lively coterie — but she was annoyed to be paid less than the men and occasionally had to sit at a 'ladies' table of wives and not among contributors.

Margit Kaffka needed to be tough socially. One of her editors, Anna Lesznai's rich cousin Lajos Hatvany, a great patron of poets, had no understanding of her problems. He was contemptuous of her untidy flat. If she did manage to tidy it, her son immediately made it into a mess again. This little boy would also interrupt serious discussions: 'Poor Margit!', Hatvany wrote condescendingly. In 1956 when he published his book of photographs and memoirs of the literary houses of Budapest, Kaffka is the only woman included among the host of male writers. Anna Lesznai wrote affectionately:

> Those Sunday afternoons of long ago at the little apartment in Márvány Street! Boxes and trunks in the hall, a worn out chiffon curtain flutters in the rush of cold air. It's dark inside but from the end of the corridor warmth of light and sound filter back. Someone rushes out to answer the bell: impossible to guess who that might be, because every Sunday brings enthusiastic visitors. One

> thing is sure: it has to be a writer, painter, artist, scholar, concerned for the paths of the spirit. Inside it's over heated, making one think of a country postmaster's room! Homemade pastries fill a large tray. We sit in a circle — the oil light flickers among eyes of lively young people, tracking the flow of ideas: they eat, listen, argue. They eat what Margit has baked, listen to her words — try to convince her in passionate argument. . . . At Margit's everyone relaxes: feels at peace.

Budapest at this time was the thriving capital city of a Habsburg Kingdom much larger than present day Hungary and in close contact with the Secession Vienna of Klimt, Freud, Wittgenstein, just up the Danube. Its cultural life was proudly Hungarian yet part of the European avant-garde. Successful plays from Budapest were translated and performed abroad — as for instance *Liliom* by Molnár which has resurfaced now as *Carousel.* People from every class or background met there. It was possible fairly cheaply to be a perpetual student, travelling all over Europe in search of the new. There were salons of intellectuals, a Galileo circle and a Sunday circle meeting to discuss and solve the problems of a changing world. They were more earnest than Bloomsbury. The diaries of Anna Lesznai show how important they considered the concept of psychological 'honesty' among friends. The 'new woman' was of course a topic for discussion and rather disturbing to the male establishment. 'Traditional women' were part of the scene as mistress, muse, assistant, a wife in the background: especially admired and adored were the actresses, opera divas and dancers.

Kaffka wrote short stories about these women who achieved financial independence but suffered many unfulfilled dreams and impossibly difficult choices.

She particularly appreciated a review at that time from George Lukács. He had understood her concern with women's issues, even though she had avoided being too specific. From her own experience she could understand conventional dismay about the 'new woman' in Ibsen and Shaw. 'For me, a young country servant girl radiating vitality meant more as a woman than all the Mme de Staels, George Sands, Selma Lagerlofs and Margit Kaffkas put together,' wrote Ernö Szabó (a one time friend).

Kaffka explored the complexities facing different generations of these new women in three novels, of which the first, *Colours and Years*, catapulted her to success. Old Magda (aged fifty), an unwanted widow in a tiny apartment, remembers. This technique of the 'talking head' unconsciously revealing her own character, her background and history, while prattling away, seemed at that time startlingly original. Recently it has been used effectively by such writers as Alan Bennet and Arnold Wesker. Magda had been forced to gamble her life on men and marriage — there seemed no choice; she had to learn by hard experience that the old role models of mother and grandmother were misleading. Magda, belle of the ball in her youth, disillusioned by husbands, afraid of vulgar sinful Budapest, is defeated into tired acceptance of her fate. Her old society was crumbling and doomed. The novel in fact chronicles the decline and corruption of her own gentry class, Church and Army are represented by the two brothers of the heroine. The family's hopes for a high position for one brother as a prince of the Church are dashed as the priest becomes ever more unstable and ends up in an asylum. (The other brother in the Army takes to drink, philandering, gambling and debts.) The daughters, whom Magda struggled to educate, neglect her; she still hopes their lives may be better than her own.

Kaffka's sure touch astonished the critics of this first novel. *The Years of Mary* followed. Mária (perhaps Magda's daughter from the earlier book) has qualifications to earn a living and need not depend on marriage, but she fares no more happily than had her mother's generation — if anything even worse. As a member of the brightest set at the college in Budapest she is full of fun and hope, her imagination absorbed by love of literature. Back home, a schoolteacher in a provincial town, she yearns for high romance. She corresponds with a famous writer in Budapest. Conflict develops between her literary fantasies, and the wretched possibility of marriage to a dreary teaching colleague. After a final attempt to discover fulfilment in the capital city, she jumps from a bridge into the Danube. The great hope, based on a modern education for women, has led only to disaster.

Her third novel, *Állomások* (*Stations*), was a *roman-à-clef* and many characters from Kaffka's circle are recognizable, including Anna Lesznai as the Jewish woman Tekla, whose character mixes in this book with her own. Margit Kaffka is bemused by the many young second generation assimilated Jews (so prominent in Budapest intellectual life), their social backgrounds, racial self-consciousness, cultural ambitions. She captures the idiom of their speech, occasional hints of Yiddish and some German. She watches with fascination the working of the system: parties, patronage, jealousies — and men harassing women. . . . She reports on chattering journalists with theories for social change. Hungarians had to be fluent in many languages and were ever avid for foreign literature, busy translating everything that was fashionable in other countries. In this novel the bright young women read

Whitman, James, Beardsley, Wilde and have *The Studio* lying on their coffee tables.

By this time Kaffka had grown a little bit more hopeful about new women, their need for compromise and sacrifice. Although Éva, when offered work and security by the Church — on condition that she dedicate her art to painting and designing exclusively for them and renounce the outside world — rejects this unctuous and odious suggestion (hypocrisy and false piety irritated Margit), she does forfeit her love life for the sake of work and a peaceful independence. Tekla, a rich and passionate Jewess, indulges her need for love at the expense of her own creativity which is offered to the man she adores. The novel ends with an exchange of long letters between these two friends explaining their choices, which are summarized in the chapter headings — 'Turbulent' for Tekla, 'Reflective' for Éva.

Margit Kaffka was concerned with social problems and injustice but believed in literature rather than politics. She had witnessed the suppression by the authorities of a peaceful socialist demonstration in May 1912. This affected her views profoundly: she wrote about it in *Stations* and in a famous rallying poem, 'Hajnali Ritmusok' ('Rhythms of Dawn'), calling on men to involve women in revolutionary change — not merely expect them to be mothers who wait patiently and fearfully at home. She had empathy with the lowest of the low in Budapest life, the women servants. She wrote particularly well about the helplessness of illiterate workers.

Literary women have often married younger men — Elizabeth Barrett, George Eliot and Dorothy Richardson come to mind. Anna Lesznai chose a friend of her eldest son, seventeen years younger than herself, for her third husband.

In 1914 Margit Kaffka aged thirty-four fell in love properly for the first time in her life. Ervin Bauer, ten years younger, was about to qualify as a doctor; and he was Jewish. His parents, both dead, had been intellectuals, lovers of literature, impoverished teachers in remote places. Marriage to a Jew was at first shocking for her family, while the difference in their ages worried Ervin's older brother who as his guardian wanted to withhold consent. As chance would have it, Margit and Ervin had met for the first time at the Lesznai country estate, Körtvélyes — a setting which many of her friends recorded in their paintings. Rippl Ronai's picture of the garden is on permanent exhibition at the National Gallery in Budapest.

Margit Kaffka was happy at last. She wrote jubilant love poetry. They enjoyed a blissful journey to Italy, but world history interrupted their idyll; in Perugia they heard of 'la guerra'. In a state of shock they returned to Budapest and got married a few weeks later. Ervin passed his examinations and had to enlist as a doctor.

War in 1914 was generally welcomed in Hungary. Kaffka was a lone voice amidst an almost universal patriotic fervour sweeping the country. In poetry and prose she cried out in despair. Alone at Christmas 1914, she wrote a poem, 'Imádkozni Próbáltam' ('I Tried to Pray'), only published in 1918, asking God to take pity on the suffering of the women. In 'Záporos Folytonos Levél' ('A Long Stormy Letter') she first describes the vast horde of anonymous poor young men tramping in the fog and the cold, in monotonous grey; marching to distant territory, without understanding what is happening; forced to kill, because their neighbours will do so. They must submit without compassion: 'Today I live — poor fellow he died not I!' Then she turns to the women, praying, lonely, desperate. Finally her personal disbelief, this CANNOT be happening to us, as individuals, you my lover and I. Love like death must be immortal.

Her story, 'Két Nyár' ('Two Summers'), from 1916, was about the reality of war coming to Budapest. It starts as a quiet leisurely tale, sympathetic to the urban poor, of a washerwoman and her unemployed husband who take a young lodger, all living their unpretentious lives. The husband is called up, the lodger expects his baby. Vera, duty bound goes to the clinic to help look after her husband's child. She reflects on women fated to give birth in travail and pools of blood:

> . . . and so a surplus of tiny bundles of steaming bodies; in order that some lives from the womb might always survive all those destined to be exterminated with most terrible weapons, in an infinite variety of bloody ways after twenty, a hundred, a thousand years to come. Thus there will always be an endless multitude of murderers and the accumulating dust of individual souls born to be destroyed in unimaginable numbers.

The reader had in no way been prepared for this sudden outcry.

Even a children's book, *Kis Emberek Barátacskáim* (*To My Little Friends*), written in 1917, instilled her pacifist message. . .

> this terrible war is the fault of grown ups: don't let it spoil your hearts or your joy forever! . . . Prepare for life *with play* because playing is for you a serious matter: True it is voluntary, no one forces you, for that would make it worthless, but play is such a good activity because from it you learn

> most and know yourself best. Prepare in this for your future, which will be better and more useful than ours now; those whom we now call enemies you will again be able to feel are friends, learn from them and work for their benefit.

She continues with chapters of practical and imaginative advice — how to make better toys at home than could be found in shops, how to make a puppet theatre, suggestions for plays, how to produce one's own newspaper and play Robinson Crusoe.

Kaffka spent the war years pushing herself to the limit, more frantically busy than ever, queuing for food, anxious for news, following her army husband to his hospital postings, in addition to her writing and teaching. (It was some consolation to her that Ervin was tending the sick, not involved in the killing.)

In 1916 while visiting her husband at his hospital in Temesvár (now Romania) Margit Kaffka wrote *The Ant Heap*. She wanted to earn enough money to buy him a Zeiss microscope for his work. Nostalgically she turned back to the most formative years of her girlhood, to the convent life she had known so well twenty years before. Maturity had mellowed her bitter memories: in *The Ant Heap* Kaffka deals gently with most of the convent motifs she had explored earlier. The teacher trainee pupils in the novel are old enough and better able to look after themselves than the young heroine of 'Letters from a Convent'. Sexual awareness is taken as common knowledge. So too are the temptations of the priests for their pupils, and the nuns' passions for each other. Even more than the splendidly depicted nuns or their precocious pupils, the convent itself becomes the centre of her story. It is an affectionate, humorous account of six months in a small community. The old Reverend Mother dies, the nuns have to elect a new head of house — it might be of an Oxbridge college. The convent becomes a microcosm of life, portrayed refreshingly without sentimentality or vulgarity.

The first chapter of *The Ant Heap* could be read as a short story of its own — of the pear which has dropped in the garden of the nunnery, and the young girls so tempted but not daring to eat it. Perhaps the nuns are testing their self-discipline? Juicy sensuous pears represent the fruit of the Garden of Eden. The novel ends in a mood of hope: gradual change and compromise are better paths to modernization than violent upheavals. Worldly politics and society are reflected in the convent. The old pioneer German nuns will have to give way to the younger progressive Hungarian nuns. Modern readers of *The Ant Heap* might find the number of orphans, whether as nuns or pupils, excessive, but this was an accurate reflection of the times, and everywhere convents were useful places for unwanted girls. Still today we are shocked by conditions for orphans in late twentieth-century Romania. Convent education might seem to ignore the secular world in which pupils will make their lives, but the bright young girls do learn what they need to know in that sisterhood.

Today's readers may also be surprised by the role and presence of priests in that community; and the amount of science taught does seem more than was usual in Anglo Saxon countries. The science teacher in *The Ant Heap*, old Father Szelényi, represents Margit Kaffka's own understated vision of religion. Magdolna, the American nun, old enough to decide on her vocation, wise enough to feel secure in her faith, is not only Sister Virginia's ideal but also that of Margit Kaffka. (Amusingly, at the beginning of this century, the author, sensitive to significant detail, had spotted the American way of smiling by showing white teeth, for it was not the fashion in conventional Hungary.) Sister Virginia trying to calm herself with prayer realizes as does Claudio in Hamlet that 'words without thoughts never to heaven go'.

Margit Kaffka pays tribute in *The Ant Heap* to the healing power of the ancient prayers at a funeral, and could share the girls' love of the Blessed Virgin Mary. She had great respect for many nuns and their achievements, while perceiving that in spite of their best efforts they may not be so different from the rest of the world as they and others liked to believe. She seemed particularly sad about nuns who entered convents without real vocations and then did not have the energy to get out: the subject of her short story 'Sister Anuncio'.

The Ant Heap appeared first in instalments in *Nyugat* during 1917 and then was published in book form the same year. The drawing on the cover of the first edition was of the threatening male intruder terrifying the young nun, her face dramatically lit up by her candle. The price was 3 koronas 50 filler. Margit Kaffka's memories of convent life were factual: about the tedium of the long services, the coldness of the stone for kneeling, the stale air and smell, cruel punishments, passionate feelings of lesbian love and much hypocrisy between preaching and practice. To convey this she uses techniques similar to those of modern documentary television: a cinema vérité portrait of an institution with shifting focus upon significant moments. Some critics were shocked by Kaffka's rational view of religion and sexuality, calling it a blasphemous and pornographic book and it has since been read as an attack on the Church in the tradition of the French enlightenment. But she also wrote with a poetic understanding of the religious life and an enjoyment of beauty in colour, music and religious symbols. Of course, the novel was a success and already reprinted the following year. In modern Hungary there is a paperback published as a set book for students.

Also in 1918, *Nyugat* published *As élet útján* (*On Life's Journey*), a slim volume of her own selection of her poems. It included a full range from some juvenilia and new poems written for Ervin. Margit Kaffka had become one of *Nyugat*'s most highly regarded authors. These war time first editions, on poor faded paper are poignant still.

After four years the long nightmare of war ended, her husband Ervin was released from military service and was able to return to Budapest from the far provinces. But Kaffka felt worried by news of the ominous Spanish flu. At the hospital, Ervin had to perform autopsies. Her son seemed at risk at his boarding school. 'If we can survive the war none of us should succumb to a silly epidemic. . . . No more army, hospital, rural isolation, bug infested messy rooms, constant journeys in over-crowded trains. There will be peace and order. And work.' In late November 1918, she was planning to research and write her first historical novel to be set in biblical times, discussed terms, advances, deadlines with her publisher. She estimated how many pages she would have to write to earn enough money for a new dress! Without realizing it she was already sickening — experiencing the early symptom of headaches — with the disease sweeping through war ravaged Europe. She died of it on the first day of December 1918; her only son died on the following day — a double tragedy. She was only thirty-eight years old with an impressive corpus of stories, novels, criticism, school books, volumes of poetry published; all achieved while working at full time jobs, running her household and looking after her son.

The shock of Kaffka's sudden death just as life beckoned was like one of the unexpected shocking endings in her own stories. A joint burial for mother and son was arranged and fellow Hungarian writers paid their tributes. Ten years later the critic, Aladar Schopflin, wrote of it:

> At the height of the struggle and panic and catastrophe of war, the horror of Spanish flu, in the city shivering with cold, in that leaden, rainy depressing December twilight, Margit Kaffka's funeral at the cemetery pierced our hearts with numbing pain — even today horror grips me when I think of it during a sleepless night. I realized then for the first time the terrible truth of death. Everything is dying now, was my feeling. . . .

Anna Lesznai wrote:

> Latterly we saw little of each other. I could only catch glimpses in short snatched meetings of the Margit who had 'arrived'. Once she had been so happy, scarcely aware of what she wrote and then her finest poems were born. At other times she feared for her happiness with such frenzy that she cried night and day: that was when she wrote 'Two Summers' the masterpiece of her despair. Then, the last time, her life seemed so orderly that she had no time for herself; only the wounds of the world hurt her. Then she departed — her soul was fulfilled.

Endre Ady had written in May that year: 'Let us rejoice in Margit Kaffka because she has arrived and proves the triumph of Hungarian feminism: one need not be polite, pay false compliments to her. She is a strong person, an artist with an assured future: no criticism can hinder her true destiny, the path marked as her own.' It is said he cried for three days on hearing of her death.

The quantity and quality of her written work was astonishing. Hungarians have continued to be proud of her, to write biographies, publish her letters, print school editions and discuss the nature of her art: a feminist writer who did not antagonize. Like other good-humoured women of any period or land — Sei Shonagun in tenth-century Japan, or Jane Austen in nineteenth-century Britain — she could transcend her milieu by artistry and human understanding. The language barrier has prevented Margit Kaffka, acclaimed as a genius by generations of her own compatriots, from reaching a wider public. Amidst the babel of gender studies, fearless unstrident feminine voices need to be treasured.

NOTE ON THE TRANSLATION

My aim has been to produce a pleasant readable modern English version rather than an annotated text edition of period Hungarian.

I have retained much of Margit Kaffka's punctuation, for example the frequent (perhaps feminine) use of the exclamation mark. I have changed the lengths of her sentences whenever this seemed easier for English comprehension. I have pruned some of her piled-on-top-of-each-other adjectives as these are irritating to the English ear. The occasional use of the present tense does not suit English literary style. Hungarian purists, perhaps, will not forgive such liberties. I agonized over the opening chapter which is deliberately 'poetic' but which translated accurately seemed silly in English today. Margit Kaffka was using the conventions of her time, the fertility of trees and nature, to write frankly about sex.

Hungarian is a more sentimental language than English. Not even a mature woman nearing seventy years can be addressed without a friendly 'my little' suffix to her name. For a Hungarian to call Jane plainly Jane would be rude. 'Hunglish' has been the source of affectionate mockery for my five English sons recalling the conversation of their grandmother and great aunt. I have not wanted Kaffka to be mocked, or to raise smiles for any other reason than her own sharp wit.

Since my marriage to an English man the challenge of translating the true meaning of Hungarian into good non-irritating English has been with me — for over forty years. My hope is that Margit Kaffka's voice will be appreciated.

ONE

September's gold had settled over this large, lovely old garden, and all neighbouring gardens and the town. No notion of chastity held back the great trees which had danced at the Feast of the Virgin and nursed tiny seeds in green cradles. Now the autumn reckoning had arrived offering everything *ad majorem dei gloriam*: ripe large fruit, lemon-yellow pears and round red apples hanging heavy on their stems. The convent garden was filled with a scent of mellow fruitfulness — so different from piercing prudish incense!

That smell of incense was nauseating in the dim corridors of the main building, where a cheerless blend of other smells, caraway soup, acorn coffee and washing-up, lingered in the cramped passage from the convent chapel to the refectory door by the huge kitchen. On these sleepy early mornings, the young girl boarders filed to breakfast after a long mass: weary, hungry, a little dazed by the mechanical uniformity of their lives, trudging silently in pairs.

At such times the great convent gate and chapel porch were open so that secular worshippers and the day pupils could enter. Daily mass was not compulsory for the latter, but they knew their reports would benefit if they looked eager. They tried to be seen by those nuns who taught them, if only in the outer courtyard, towards the end during the reading of the Gospel. They touched their irreverent young foreheads with a few drops of Holy Water, shivering, profanely, in a hurry. Meanwhile, the boarders in blue uniforms could inhale for a brief moment the happy secular scent of outer air.

Their eager eyes saw a stretch of the town street. Misleadingly as in a dream, and briefly, there was life as they had once known it — last year, the year before, at home. In their villages where they had gone to school from their parents' houses, mothers had woken them, scolded them if they lazed in bed, combed their hair; and they remembered the aroma of real coffee. With satchels they had hurried along the sunny streets, shouting at boys, laughing, shoving each other with their elbows. Mari with her large basket had gone off to market. And here at the chapel entrance one might see such girls with baskets, old women with rosaries, a few bare-headed young students who ministered at services and were keen for a place in the priests' quarters. They saw the day girls, the lucky ones who came from their own homes to convent school, but only knew them by name. In class the girls in uniform had to sit on separate benches, communication with the worldly ones was in effect forbidden, limited to the politeness of 'sisterly love'.

At the end of mass the little profane girls would stand aside, looking on with embarrassed curiosity as the formal line filed past. The great freedom of careless days induced a kind of respect for ritual order, for lives bound by strict rhythm. These girls watching the nuns and novices giggled together a bit enviously.

Most conspicuous was the old fat red-faced nun. They knew she was the terror of her dark blue flock. Kunigunda, *gumi bunda!*— they mocked and tittered behind her back. Well, they were outside the circle of her power. How she hated them, not even troubling to look back. She would not have been able to pick out the guilty one, had no authority over them; but her large face flushed deeper red from anger, and her thick hand clenched the carved skull-bead of her rosary. 'Untidy! Ragamuffins! Riffraff!' she shouted with a bad German accent in her rough masculine voice. Her large back shut out the day girls' view of the street; the dangerous stimuli of morning sunshine, movement, freedom. '*Hur-ry*!' she kept rasping until the sleepy walking column was sucked into the narrow corridor at the side. And woe betide anyone at such a time who whispered so much as a word in her neighbour's ear, or broke the morning's *silenceum* with even a gesture. If it were a young pupil she would have to kneel in the middle of the refectory as punishment; if an older girl, she would have to listen for minutes on end to compelling sergeant-like nagging, jarring her nerves, in the oppressive quiet.

With that the day began: the work periods, lessons, exercises, religious instruction, communal prayers, litany to the point of fainting, kneeling on the cold stone — exactly the same day after day. Of course, they could get used to the 'Old One', and during prayers thoughts could fly away, but this awful monotony. . . . For the days of youth are so terribly long, so restless the waiting, and impatient the longing for life.

Yet there was the garden — sweet-scented and beautiful. It was so nice to come here, leave the painfully clean day parlour, the dim passageways, paved courtyards; to pass the new school buildings and the gardener's cottage, along the end of the large dull kitchen garden and the path between the gooseberry bushes; at last to arrive by the wire fence into a world of shade, where they no longer had to trudge along in that terrible paired crocodile. They could spread out on the leafy twisting paths, or hide by the wooden fence in the lilac thicket. Here during the afternoon, while the weather was fine, the little primary and middle-school children could play hide-and-seek for a few hours, while older girls shared secrets, or mused in private.

For here the grass was not scented with pious incense or sad smoke, and the trees were not at all bashful, though it was a convent garden. In the summer months they were busy with their swelling fruits. Now that autumn had returned and the noisy little virgin humans under their shade were chirping and longing for their warm nests at home . . . now the large lemon-yellow pears were ready, over-ripe, hanging by their stems waiting for just a tiny breeze, and. . . .

'Puff!'

'Look how big it is! Phew!'

'If I were at home now I'd pick it up and bite it and *schlupp*! Oh the juice would just slurp out.'

Three little girls stopped their game of 'mourning rites', which was a traditional pastime in September; the children, especially if they were new, would sit together on a bench, and would cry in turn with sweet deep delight. They would recall the happiness of the homes they had left behind, their precious little past lives; and compete — in an extraordinarily adult and instinctively Christian way — extolling all its beauties. . . .

And now a large, over-ripe pear had dropped! But it had to be left there on the ground, or perhaps reported to Sister Kunigunda, and taken over to her. Then it would reach the preserving room or perhaps the kitchen. Maybe they would stew it with a little sugar for the sick in winter: yes, because that is the rule . . . and it was only the Devil putting temptation into people's way . . . and they would burn in Hell or go to Purgatory; and that would be bad enough, but Sister Kunigunda would create so, perhaps even put the red badge of shame on one's back, and how she would shout. Oh dear! If only one could pick it up secretly — but three people had noticed, perhaps others too. That Janka Wester would surely tell, because she was related to one of the nuns; and two senior girls were watching them from behind a tree, smiling . . . and, even if no one knew it, at the Last Judgement it would come out because every sin is recalled then, and people are shamed, isn't it so? Even confessed sins come out into the light, but for those you won't feel shame in your heart — isn't that true?

Slowly, trembling they got nearer the point of temptation. There on the grass all yellow . . . what a thrill, what danger, the precious promise of all earthly joys, sin of desire, temptation of the taste buds! Oh innocent fruit of the tree! How huge, swollen, what a maliciously poisoned mix of fantasy and prohibition! The seed of the tree, God's fruit. Now truly Satan was smiling at the amber-coloured beauty. . . . You have taken the sins of the world upon you!

'Vats das? Pick up and eat her! Na . . . vat, vas you say? You silly geese!'

Caught by surprise the three little ones froze in terror. What's happening? It was she, the dreaded Kunigunda, approaching from behind. In her hands the rosary had ceased moving, her mouth stopped its eternal soundless mumbling. She looked at the little ones and on her large simple red countenance appeared a rare visitor, a strange shy smile; a little profane, a little maternal perhaps — something of understanding, a reminiscence of long ago. . . . The next minute she retreated, rather embarrassed, to her usual irritability. The little ones could hardly believe their ears. Hesitatant and nervous, they approached the fruit. The nun turned away, still muttering something. Her heavy figure with its stern features disappeared with rare speed along the curve of the path. She went towards the exit.

'Are we allowed to eat it?' asked a little blonde girl with a comb in her hair, still pale from fright. 'Can it be true?' They stood in a huddle, uncertain and shivering. They held the beautiful fruit in their hands.

Janka Wester joined them. Until now she had regarded them stiffly with the sickly gaze of her large intrusive eyes. Her pale face was partly hidden by an open geography book from which she had been swotting.

'No, don't eat it. I wouldn't advise it. Sister was just testing your self-denial. Come with me, down there by the fence in the trunk of that big tree, our class has a Lourdes statue. We got it at our First Holy Communion. Offer it for the honour of the Blessed Virgin Mary. Let's go and give it to Her. You will be repaid ten fold in Heaven. Of course, you are not allowed to touch the altar, because our class bought the silk and the holy pictures. But if you want to offer something you can give it to me!'

'Oh yes, that will be good,' said the little blonde girl, trembling from agitation, happy with the honour to be bestowed. 'And I have a lovely picture of the Sacred Heart in a lace frame, and I'll offer that as well!' she added suddenly enthusiastic about the idea that over there in Heaven she will receive ten framed lace pictures in return. And so they started off led by the tall lanky teenager, with the beautiful fruit held aloft for a ritual offering. In the hollow of the ancient tree, by the white feet of the Madonna of Lourdes, hungry caterpillars and tiny maggots could look to a merry banquet. For the lowliest creatures are equally in God's care.

TWO

The two senior girls laughed.

'Did you see that?'

'What's happened to the Old One? A miracle? Has she gone mad?'

'Not at all. Just look along the road. Look who is coming.'

'Aha, it's Virginia, now I understand. Love can turn tigers into doves.'

'Oh stop it, I hate that sort of thing.'

A slender girl of rather special beauty, with long wavy brown hair, was saying this while leaning close to the other who was smooth faced and fair haired with intelligent eyes. She had a full figure and well-developed hips and bust. Both were in their final year.

'Now look here my little wife,' laughed the mature blonde, 'two years ago you were running after the beautiful Sister Bernarda.'

'That was then. Shut up here for years one still has a

heart — or as you say, imagination. Consciously or unconsciously one picks up this nonsense. But you've put me straight since you arrived last year.'

'Your fascinating cousin the painter sorted you out during the summer holidays last year, little wife. Portrait, trellis bower, moonlight, your uncle's garden in the village, and all the stories about Paris he stuffed into your little head.'

'Leave me in peace, Erzsi, honestly. You know Victor and I are no longer friends, since all we did this summer was quarrel and annoy each other. Everything is finished. Even my uncle the priest noticed us. He told us relatives should live in peace and love — and now, although my cousin has written to me once through your friend who brings letters, I am not answering. It's finished.'

'Everything is over. I wonder? Cornelia, you hot little Romanian, you've done well. Only eighteen and already you've got a past — hot kisses (well almost!) in the rose bower, an eventful summer and a faithless whim. Of course, our teacher Kapossy is an interesting priest, even if he isn't handsome. His eyes are fiery like Savanarola's. He holds his cassock like a cloak above his knees when he lectures with passion about Pestalozzi, as if he himself had crushed the serpent's head by blowing with heavenly gentleness into the nostril of the beggar's child. . . . Perhaps he is right and these are the important things in the world — but in a convent it's difficult to accept it. Anything big gets suffocated here by thousands of weird and wonderful details.'

'How interested you are in all these ideas, Erzsi! That's what amazes me. Someone as clever as you who knows life so well. In your place I wouldn't be able to stand it, I wouldn't live in. How can you bear the monotonous boredom?'

'It's cheaper for my mother if I live as a boarder. Apart from that, it's a reassuring thought for someone (my special friend), you know, the one I mentioned to you. And after all, there's lots to amuse me here. Interesting things happen everywhere, if you know how to observe them and not get involved.'

'Yes but you were once immersed in *life*. . . .'

'In *life,* my dear! Perhaps you think it's more amusing to be a girl, a girl living at home? When I finished secondary school my father was still alive. I was kept at home, and taken out to balls. A home dressmaker sewed my gowns, that was all right, it was fun. I was courted by my father's colleagues and my brother's fellow officers. Sometimes I was serenaded at night. If I stuck my head out of the window to shake the dusters out while cleaning, a beau might be waiting; in the evenings I might allow my hand to be kissed. They gossiped in the town. All that's quite amusing, once or twice, but then it gets boring. I was considered a poor girl so my only proposal came from a pharmacist past his prime. Father died and mother's pension was tiny, but she was clever and inventive. She started a business offering home-cooked meals, it was good and cheap for bachelors. In the evenings we would play the piano and have fun. Sometimes they stayed around till midnight. Well, then the town really started to gossip! They said terrible things about us. My poor mother cried when just a little of it got back to her ears.

'It was around then that I got to know our Member of Parliament. Yes . . . that's right, it was to do with my mother's pension, and I asked for his help. I put on my nice tight-fitting brown velvet dress. I talked and joked with him, the whole thing was fun for me, I was bored, I was twenty. I admired a dark red rose in his garden; the next morning his gardener brought me a cart full. And so it went on . . . I could see he was hooked; his rich wife had been ill for five years, she could hardly get out of her chair. And this MP is a handsome man, has seen the world, is clever — I learnt a lot from him. Lord knows, somehow the thing became more serious, I got caught up in it too; and he found me surprising and interesting — did not wish me any harm, or to ruin my life. He's a nice ageing romantic idealist! So we struggled, dreamed; the small town gossiped of course, my mother was shocked.

'Then together we made a plan. I should study and become independent, he would see about a job for me. After six years of secondary school they take you on as a third-year trainee, and the diploma only takes two years. I've completed one, in ten months I shall be finished. By that time the new school in the town will have been built and I shall be the Headmistress right away. After all, he was the founder and got the state grant. If you want to, my dear, by this time next year, you can teach there too, under my jurisdiction. When our school "develops" with higher classes, we can also acquire the higher qualifications needed for them. Yes, higher salaries; greater independence — that's a good thing. You can't accept money from someone, specially if you are in love with him. This way it's all quite satisfactory. Perhaps something may happen for him too. Maybe he'll find a place in a sanatorium for his poor wife. I'm twenty-two now, which isn't old, my angel. Only you eighteen-year-olds think it old. Oh, compared to him, I'm still too young. If you knew what nice letters he writes. They are so entertaining and in classical literary style. So, with all this in view, surviving this last year is possible, and to make time pass quicker I watch all the amusing characters here. It's no different, only life in miniature; amoebas in a drop of water, as a fashionable writer put it.'

The darker girl sighed.

'Truly Erzsi I admire you, your sense, your calm, your mood. And what surprising phrases you use. Not every twenty-two-year-old expresses herself like you do, believe me. Perhaps it doesn't depend on the fact that you lived at home so long, as a débutante. You need to be born wise. Oh, how much one can learn from you. It's true I never lived in a town. My uncle, the priest, put me into this convent straight from our village, and I have been here for five years, and always spent vacations back in the village . . . but in any case I was born timid; they say that's what Romanian women are like. They say my poor dear mother, who died so young I never knew her, couldn't even buy dress material for herself. She dreaded going into shops, and having to bargain was most embarrassing for her. She was miserable in company. Often when they went to a church meeting in town, she would escape from all the people and sit in the garden, where she could be in peace. I take after her in character, although physically I've grown tall like my late father and his brother my uncle. . . . I don't think I shall ever be independent. How will I ever learn to withdraw money, pay for a home and food, do my housekeeping? Honestly, I haven't the slightest idea what ten koronas is worth, or what you can buy with it. I'll have to stay and become a nun, if you don't help me. Here I know what to do — the bell rings: there is the food. It rings again: get into pairs, go here, go there, get up, lie down according to the clock.'

'You are so bored by it all, you crazy little thing!'

'Terribly! But I'm bored with everything, even the breathing we have to do continually. . . I wonder if anything will ever happen in my life. It would just have to come to me, as I can't arrange love like you. In your place I would die from jealousy, and be worried by gossip and the future. Oh my God!'

She spoke wearily, supporting her young figure against the tree.

'Well, of course you can't live like this, my dear,' said the other thoughtfully, quietly. 'Are you anaemic? It wouldn't be surprising here. I was like that a few years ago, and it can lead to trouble, if you don't stand up for yourself and take a firm hold on life. Live, observe, enjoy while you can. The whole thing might be short. Don't make too much of a tragedy of anything. Look over there at the old priest among the cabbages with his grey umbrella, nice old Father Szelényi, look at him! He's really sensible. He only observes the world. He doesn't have love affairs, doesn't want promotion, mumbles to himself in the physics lab among his instruments, walks about with a big cigar, smiling; and everything that's happening interests him, he knows it all and is not shocked by anything.'

'Yes, you're that type too.'

'Don't forget, my friend, that if I'm observing and sniffing around it's mainly so that I can report these convent entertainments at night, in secret, carefully, in a pencilled letter to Budapest — to my sweet old gentleman friend who is fascinated by all these psychological phenomena and enchanted by my style and worldly views. I'm not yet at the really wise stage; but believe me that being like this is the only way that one can survive here. Or like Marika Pável who immerses herself in novels so she can act them out, and is constantly at the forefront of all gossip. Look at her, what has she seen of life? Her widower father is a station master in some impossible place. She has been here for eight years and she has had a romance with every priest who teaches here. She has been in every sort of trouble. She has gone to all the different wings of the buildings at night just for the hell of it. She has been the heroine of inquisitions, and has accomplices and rivals in love. She'd never have such an exciting busy life outside — unless she were a student actor. But it is more amusing like this.

'Do you know what she did yesterday? She went along the corridor to her piano lesson, her music under her arm, her cloak open, red like a rose. She went up to the floor above the house chapel where, at that time, Jóska Fóth usually ministers to our sick Reverend Mother. He is the handsome instructor of theology, Marika only likes them if they are good looking. They met and smiled, stopped close to one another, one looked up, the other down, had the same thought and, in a moment, *smack* they kissed and then ran away panting. What do you think? Isn't that something? On a bright Sunday morning in the corridor of the convent, in front of Reverend Mother's room, Marika had a great kiss with the Chaplain, and the walls did not collapse on her, and the oil burner by St Vincent's blackened picture flickered steadily on. That is how you have to live, my dear, if you don't want to be mummified. You can't just get het up in secret and mooch around and gaze at the stars because your hero has talked about eclipses during physics. You haven't even got as far as handing him the exercise books for correction at the end of the lesson. You could leave meaningful notes between the pages, broken sighs, significant words, pencil drawn hearts with two rubbed out names; and you'd get some reply in the margins, or he'd suggest you see him after the lesson in the staff room, and would talk to you seriously, in a quiet stifled way, hiding his rising curiosity. "But my dear young lady! . . ." He would be embarrassed, you would cry, he would lean towards you and hold your hand. . . . And then?'

'Oh Erzsi! That's all so silly, so childish and shaming . . . such tricks!'

'But I assure you, it's no different out there in so-called real life, the hunt for men. Only the means are different, here it's rather adolescent — tried out on nun catching. Take Szidu and Gidu for example. Those two are now running after young Emerika. They always share their idol. The other day, in the empty art room I saw that name flourished on the blackboard in splendid calligraphy and surrounded by garlands of grapes and leaves. Those two were in there and messing around for an hour, because Sister Emerika would later be giving a remedial lesson to two girls who had failed their exams. Those two understand the methods. I bet you in a year the one will be married to her father's chief assistant who will take over the chemist shop; and the other will be lucky if she is not pregnant by the town clerk of the district where she is teaching. Look, I think we should discreetly move on from here. We are disturbing an idyll!'

Laughingly Erzsi gestured towards stout Kunigunda and her guest, the tall, dark-faced nun, and led her friend in the direction of the kitchen garden.

'There is going to be such fun here this year,' Erzsi said as they hurried past the wire fence. 'Reverend Mother seems to be really ill, when she dies there will be an election. All the members of the Order who have the emblem of the skull and the right to vote will come in from sister houses all over the country. The nuns will fast here for a week before the election and pray for holy guidance. I believe secret campaigning has begun already, the little ant heap is boiling and sizzling, though from the outside you'd hardly notice. Obviously important matters are being discussed. Why would Virginia have come to talk to stupid old Kunigunda when at other times she ignores her?'

'Good Lord, what a lot you know!'

'Look over there. Helen has probably been called to

visit her sick aunt, our Reverend Mother. It must be difficult for her being a relation. Now look she has reached the cabbages. Father Szelényi has stopped her, to ask her something, as I expected. He has to know about everything. . . . He is trying to identify some newly arrived geological specimen because the label has come off. He has burnt a hole in his cassock with a drop of hydrochloric acid. He'll wear it happily, so many greasy spots on his tummy already. He doesn't care. By the way, that tame Bavarian girl is also at the centre of a great commotion. You know she has a fortune of a hundred thousand koronas, and happens to be an orphan with only a guardian living in Munich and our Reverend Mother. I think they want to work on the girl while Reverend Mother is alive. All the old dears guard her terribly.'

'You mean they want to make a nun of her? Poor thing. That's horrible.' Cornelia was shocked.

'Who knows, perhaps it would be good for her; it depends what she is like. I've tried to get to know her, but it's difficult at the moment. I do know that she has not been to a convent before. She used to live with her guardian and attended a secular school in a little German town. Well — we shall see.'

THREE

Sister Virginia was a strikingly handsome woman, well built, olive skinned, thick eyebrows over dark eyes. Her mature figure would suggest that she was about thirty years old; but it is difficult to gauge a nun's age by her face. The crisp veil of snow-white linen, starched, ironed, was always flattering since it covered signs of age: early wrinkles at the brow, misleading matronly curves of neck and chin, greying hair.

This whiteness billows back like the wide wings of a dove. The tight part, round the face, stretches the skin slightly, making it more youthful. The reflection of so much white ennobled a pale face, made a dark countenance seem more energetic and commanding, and a lively face look altogether more vigorous. The drapery, spreading down to the waist followed every idiosyncratic movement of the head and neck. Each sister could be identified from behind, as in solemn procession they advanced towards the altar in the half-lit church to receive the body of their Lord. The black habit might appear to be uniform, giving a certain calm dignity to movement, but it revealed individual traits. Adolescent pupils in their ardent admiration discussed this at length. The charm of the habit has attracted many women who were shy, unsure of themselves, alienated by the world, yet who deceived themselves into a belief in their 'calling'. Outside they had become depressed by their wretched clothes, the poor tawdry materials, badly cut; such clothes killed all self-esteem. Here they were surprised by their self-confidence and discovery of hidden qualities, helped by physical appearance. Certain gestures are peculiar to convents — unctuous, classically measured — caused by wearing the habit. Such movements looked and felt good. Perhaps this is why these women, the poor little candidates dressed in mouse-coloured striped skirts and misshapen collars, waited so earnestly to change their dress, and place the veil upon their combed hair at the year's end.

Nuns seldom remembered much of their former life; even if it had carried into adolescence. This was not merely a matter of devoutness and the compulsory casting away of worldly things; the routine here reshaped them fast. A narrow world, new concepts, compelling and different, obliterated the complex past which perhaps they had been glad to leave.

Virginia had lived in a beautiful cathedral town, where her Italian father had been part artist, part choirmaster, and she had attended a convent school, though of a different order. She was eighteen when her father died. Within a year her mother had remarried, a fencing master towards whom the young girl felt a wholly unchristian loathing. She then decided to enter a convent, far from home and her stepfather. Later as a novice she prayed often and fervently for forgiveness, with contrite sorrow, for the causeless hatred she had felt towards her mother's second husband whom, after all, she hardly knew. After a while she was comforted, convinced he had been the means by which providence had led her to her vocation. She prayed for the salvation of her family and promptly forgot them completely. All her spiritual potential and abilities were developed in the convent. She matured into a person who was totally committed to it.

In the early days, still studying for exams, she was assigned to work as supervisor of the boarders under Kunigunda and forced to put up with a lot from the old woman, who would scold her, and in front of the pupils too. It was said that Kunigunda's father had once been a forester on some large German estate. She, not he, had kept order among the thieving woodmen, drunken hunters, well able to frighten off the most aggressive poacher with her terrible tongue. A pupil who happened to come from the same part of the country had once spread such gossip, and in a convent that kind of story is passed on from generation to generation.

It was certainly true that this worthy red-faced woman kept order and cleanliness among those assigned to her care; completed her daily devotions, rosaries and penances with clockwork regularity, punctual for every service. They respected and trusted her; and, moreover, she gave her inferiors much opportunity to earn merit by patient endurance. Those who had little to do with her would be gently amused by her oddity. This loud and fearsome person had a naïve simple soul. She nursed an old houseplant in the parlour as tenderly as one might a child. It was said she was gentle and forbearing to the few orphans who remained in the convent during summer holidays, when most of the boarders enjoyed their lives in distant homes. During the unaccustomed quiet she would mourn for the nuns who had died long ago, and talk affectionately of their ways. At other times a primitive curiosity overcame her. She would call the little girls to herself one by one, and grill the unsuspecting child about her home, her parents, her circumstances. She became a village woman again, unsophisticated and prejudiced, who by insinuation made the children admit that life in the world outside was terrible: universal poverty, bad marriages, husbands beating wives, relatives jealous. . . . 'Ja-ja, so ist die Welt,' she would say, well satisfied, and release the terrified girl. If later this child dared fuss about food, leaving the tough German turnip on her plate, she would bark unpleasantly at her,'At home you vould eat it, you can starve, nitwit, louse!'; flushing a shade darker and watching until the poor child had forced down the uneatable food, only then would she walk on, mumbling, and click one bead of her rosary. She was like that.

Virginia, as a beautiful young nun, soon discovered what lay behind the Old One's nagging rages and military personality: a secret shy passion of which she, Virginia, was the object. At first Virginia responded slightly but this awkward devotion which obsessed the older nun became burdensome. Later, when the pupils and other nuns observed this state of affairs with amusement, Virginia was embarrassed, asked to be moved, and mocked the old woman like everybody else.

After working a few years in sister houses, as was the custom, she found herself back here in the provincial mother house and rapidly created a career. She was one of a few chosen for higher studies on account of her Hungarian birth and her abilities. She received lessons from local schoolmaster priests. She was sent to take the state exams so that legal requirements could be met.

The Catholic community was preparing to found new secondary schools — the former bishop, a nationally accepted star in the Church, had approved and helped these plans — and Virginia became a pillar of the scheme. In these mature years she was imbued by a passionate love of work, a fiery energy and activity. As well as her daily spiritual exercises she taught for eight hours in the Training College, dealt with the administration, corresponded and met people from the outside world, priests and staff. Her bearing was smooth, courteous, superior, affected as all Church performers, God knows where she learnt it. *Everything for the Order, and for our Country!* — this was the ideal for which she strove. She was party to all business matters; external accounts and directives from the Ministry of Education passed through her hands. She corresponded with financial institutions and with parents of the pupils; and at night she studied architectural plans for the school building along the side of the garden. She had the kind of personality which likes to throw itself into tangible and practical matters. Now the welfare and development of their Order absorbed her.

Once when she had been ill for a year, she had written their national history. This valuable little work saw the light of day in the episcopal press. She knew and loved this Order, the old mother house, the onetime barracks with closed corridors, blackened holy pictures, and the crypt below where departed former sisters rested in Christ. She loved the charming chapel, she had chanced to read about the artistic merit of the altar painting. She loved the neighbouring estates even though she never saw them, and the steep little vineyards where they sometimes went in autumn for the grape harvest. The nuns sang hymns and patriotic songs. She remembered happily one such afternoon, when she was able to recite her daily prayers out in the open, under God's sky shaded by the rustling trellis of vines, and she marvelled from the depth of her soul at all the beauty of our Heavenly Father's Creation.

Here, in the rigour of the mother house, she rarely had a chance for that sort of thing; but in the sister houses, where she had spent a few years, they sometimes had excursions into the hills. The nuns might meet Catholic gentlewomen of the town who held meetings of their ladies' guild in the convent. Sometimes (with the local Reverend Mother) they might pay a visit to an older woman for a friendly secular tea. Virginia did not find anything amiss in all this . . . after all, you shouldn't have to *guard people's sanctity by force*. Her firm mouth was angry at the thought of it. Berchtolda, the new Mistress of the Novitiates, was right: 'We must not train our nuns so that they are unable to resist temptations. . . . The aim of Catholic education is solidarity with the whole Catholic world,' she had reflected sincerely. Virginia when studying the letter of foundation and the history of the Order, had found that originally it had been a shelter for religious women as much as for unmarried girls withdrawing from the world; and the task had been precisely to work, be effective, give advice, convert; to save and lead souls from sin to the path of salvation.

She was immersed in and inspired by the true spirit of her Order and had convinced herself of a purpose: to develop and raise its prestige among the other female orders. She knew them all from visitors passing through. There were poor mendicant orders whose abbesses would travel in large leather boots, wear a rough habit and go begging with a crucifix, bowl in hand, to the towns. There were orders exclusive to old noble families, or to girls with vast dowries, and when they visited they would make up their beds with coronet embroidered linen, their own trousseau.

Virginia's Order was somewhere in the middle. The nuns were recruited from the neighbouring townsfolk, minor gentry and German peasant farmers. They brought their own simple linen and a few thousand koronas, or adequate talent, to acquire the teaching diploma; they could study while working hard and long. The Order had convents in every corner of the country, and nursed in many a worldly hospital to everyone's satisfaction. With so much effort, activity and sleeping capital we ought to be more important in the life of the Church, thought Virginia. In the first instance they ought to be richer, as money was the secret of all influence and power in the world, the means to do good. With her intellect she understood this. She personally had taken a vow of poverty, hardly possessing anything other than what she was wearing. She had transferred all her own personal ambitions to her Order. She was grateful for her abilities of organization for the benefit of the Order, yes only for that reason was she pleased with her growing influence. At the beginning of the year she had been appointed 'officially' secretary to the sick Reverend Mother.

The present Reverend Mother had been elected by the old nuns, now retired. In their heyday they had obeyed her predecessor, for they had come here together. This old guard originated from a Bavarian mission. A bishop of former times had them brought here. He had sworn that even the swineherds would curse in German in this district where, until then, there had only been sporadic German villages in the midst of the uncontaminated, stubborn Hungarians. It was still possible, then, to get away with that kind of colonial mentality in Hungary, without provoking opposition. The good bishop considered the education of women important for his plan. The daughters of the gentry of that time (grandmothers of the modern young matrons), started to struggle with the German language in the convent, and learnt the famous art of stencil painting. All this good knowledge did not reach down to the swineherd, but the bishop (excellent Prince of the Church) passed into the hands of the Order substantial properties confiscated from dissidents. In the old house, the former barracks, which they had also acquired through him, new pupils had arrived once again, and new sisters trained the next generation of nuns. The old nuns, surviving witnesses of those former days, now lived in the west wing. They watched events from there and prepared themselves by prayer for the heavenly wedding. Apart from this they had no duties other than to set a good example to the young ones and preserve the strict spirit of their vows. Virginia was aware of the situation. For the moment the old nuns were watching everything without a word but with eagle eyes, resentment concealed in humility. Reverend Mother was ill. Perhaps she would soon go to Jesus.

Old Mother Leona, sister of the previous head, once put it very charmingly; 'Poor dear Virginia truly makes too great a sacrifice for our Order. For the pure love of it she makes her own spiritual struggle here on earth so hard for herself, taking upon herself all the temptations of worldliness and pride. Earthly knowledge is often the snare of the Devil.'

And there was always someone in the community who would tactfully, 'only out of love', repeat such remarks to Virginia.

FOUR

'Ah, liebe, liebe Schwester!' Purple-faced Kunigunda, trembling with embarrassment, approached. Clumsily she tied a knot in her rosary to mark the pause in her prayers. She moved, and was behaving like a young pupil caught in a naughty act, but magnified out of proportion. Despite a lack of sympathy, Virginia could not help smiling.

'What a rare visitor you are here in our boarding school,' continued the Old One in German and held out her stocky hand. 'How are you, dear Sister?'

'By the Grace of our Lord Jesus Christ, I am well,' replied the guest with ritual formality.

'You are so busy, you neglect us here, your old friends, your old home. And how is your precious health, sweet Sister?'

'Thank you, quite well now, thanks be to God.'

'For ever amen! Come and look at our garden, how beautiful it is! During the summer holiday I often used to think of our dear Sister. That perhaps you might visit us on a beautiful Sunday afternoon. I put out the chair as of old, when this garden was your home. Do you remember how we prayed together under the big tree and then talked till teatime?'

'Yes indeed!' smiled Virginia, recalling the scolding and nagging done by the shrill voice of the Old One, 'of course, everything is the same as seven years ago when I lived here. Only the lilac bushes have grown and the trees are seven years older too.'

'We ourselves were younger then!' sighed the Old One, some strange sentimental grimace on her face.

'The time of youth, the time of nonsense,' replied Virginia diplomatically. She sat down, with measured priestly movements, on the chair by the garden table.

So they talked. Although they lived under the same roof, the strictly proscribed life kept them separate, in different wings of the convent, with different duties. They hardly had any contact, as hallowed silence was the rule in the refectory while they ate together, and the chapel was the place of worship. These artificial distances were the ideal hotbed for strange fantastic ardours, usually for an isolated nun or training novice, seldom among close colleagues. The dark old house was riddled with such unmentionable absorbing attractions. Tell-tale glances while leaving the chapel, trembling hands, ethereally light but with unforgettable emotion, touching the rim of the Holy Water bowl. Or it could be a chance meeting, or a barely murmured word which might be of the deepest significance for private and uneventful lives.

However secret this might seem, such unsubstantial connections would usually be known to the whole convent. News of a new passion or faithless rejection would travel round the Order, via a nun transferred beyond the Danube, into Transylvania, to the children's home by the seaside or even to the old castle in the Carpathian Mountains where the very sick were sent for convalescence. 'Oh, I was young once!' — a middle-aged nun, who still had dreams, might sigh. The old ones would usually shake their heads with disapproval, though just as eager for gossip. Sister Simonea, who had been in charge of candidates before Berchtolda, used to tell her flock during the Friday evening dressing down: 'The corridor in a convent is the same as the street in the world outside. Any one who is out in the corridor too often and without good cause is, please remember this well, like a "street walker".' And if, at some corner or top of the stairs, creeping past the faded image of a holy martyr a happy 'chance meeting' did occur, the young novice girls would have their bleak lives filled with meaning — though hearts were beating and teeth chattering with fear. At the end of the week they earnestly confessed all such sins. Praying on the cold stone, they would atone for letting attraction to a human soul dim their devotion to God's love. Next week they would fall into sin again, and again until their youth passed. . . .

'It seems we might soon be in mourning,' started Virginia flatly, her fine white hands clasped. 'Reverend Mother took the last rites for the third time today.'

'Oh yes, such is life! Great sorrow will come to us,' replied the Old One. Her head nodded agreement, her voice was deeply indifferent. She never took part in communal affairs. She scolded, kept order, did her duty. She hardly saw Reverend Mother except to kiss her hand at high holidays in the traditional way.

For one minute both of them sat silent with suitably downcast eyes.

'Did Reverend Mother send for young Helen?' asked Kunigunda with more interest.

'Yes. I sent her up a few minutes ago, with permission. How do you find the poor girl?'

'So, so. She is a stranger here. She just drifts among the others or sits by herself — like a heap of misery.'

'She is not used to it, and perhaps she is weighed down by her aunt's illness, her only relative. Sometimes these earthly ties are strong.'

'Nonsense, she hardly knew her. Why did they have to educate her in the world! Who knows what her head is full of? And now this friendship with Mrs Holzer, what is the use of all that?'

'Excuse me, dear Sister, but that was the express wish of Reverend Mother.'

'Of course, of course. You must be right. These are your affairs. I just blow my old trumpet. Don't understand a lot of things, and I don't bother with them, but my heart still has feelings . . . yes, yes. . . .'

Virginia quickly turned her head. She did not want to see the impossible, peculiar, sloppy expression on the old nun's face. She gazed out at the leafy sunflecked green, and the moving blue-clad figures on the white paths. Seriously, convincingly, she started to explain.

'Reverend Mother considered it important her niece should only enter the convent if she feels a true vocation. She is right. She has such deep understanding, like the saints to whom we shall soon have to give up her dear company.'

'Is *that* the way you see things, dear Sister?' Kunigunda burst out. She stamped her foot agitated by the silent rebuke of a moment ago. 'You say this sort of thing, with all your experience of the outside world and all its worthless affairs? You. . . .'

'Of course I know', smoothly, smiling Virginia continued, 'the convent life is the happiest and most perfect on earth, and most likely to ensure paradise. Certainly it is a good deed to win over for our Order a soul suited for service to God. Dear Sister knows how much I approve of Sister Berchtolda's understanding of the novitiate. She has interpreted the rules more gently during the few months she has held the post.'

'Yes indeed! Such a mess there. Letting themselves go. Terrible! Eight o'clock at night, after prayers, the young novitiates are gadding around the corridors. Who ever heard of such a thing. They should have tried it during Simonea's time, she would have dealt with them. You must remember, I remember you kneeling in the corridor where the pupils go towards the dormitories, just for one loud word, and you were already a fully fledged novice. All the boarders filed past you in their pairs.'

'I have always been deeply grateful to Sister Simonea for her training in convent discipline,' replied the younger sister. Her voice was slightly muffled, and her mouth twitched nervously from the older woman's tactless remark. Kunigunda noticing, frightened, pulled herself together.

'For sure, you know all these things better. You are younger, you are the "working order", the Marthas. Now is their time. I just blow my old trumpet, but I'm not worse than others, may the dear Lord forgive me. I speak my mind, but you can speak with me, we can talk . . . yes yes, you know that, sweet Sister. We often used to sit in this garden together, while our pupils played around, and shared our thoughts, discussed the work of our Order, of the other sisters, and the whole sinful world. Do you remember?'

'And you certainly gave me a good dressing down if I was late by even half a minute for the inspections. Of course I remember!' smiled Virginia, turning into a jest the tense, impatient embarrassment which overwhelmed her, faced with unrequitable, pathetic, foolish affections.

'I wanted all your free time for me, that you should

spend it here by me . . . yes, it hurt to think you were meeting others in the corridors, or visiting them in the *regracio* hour. I knew you were in daily contact with other teaching sisters, who were better educated, cleverer than I, more suited to you! Oh! . . .' With trembling face, almost tearful eyes, she looked at Virginia imploringly.

'The time of youth, the time of nonsense, isn't that it?' parried the visitor again. 'To continue. I am very much aware how much our little Helen's joining the convent would mean to us. And above all, and most important, it could mean the salvation of her soul, with God's will. But only, dear Sister, only if she clearly feels her calling as we once felt it. Our life here has many trials, we know that don't we?'

'Oh yes yes, Dear God!'

'Reverend Mother told her in my hearing, she should not enter otherwise, better to wait. Reverend Mother wanted her to be educated outside by her guardian, to know the world first. Reverend Mother agreed she should make friends here in the town with Mrs Holzer who is after all a decent, faithful Catholic woman, President of the Catholic League for Church Vestments, and we were most beholden to her last year for the generous provision of the most beautiful things. Reverend Mother did not oppose the suggestion that Helen might go each month for a meal with that young woman, to spend her day off with a respectable family. What could be wrong in that? The other boarders go out at those times, and the poor little orphan has no one here. She might have been put off by too sudden a transition from secular life to the complete seclusion of a convent. Are you listening, dear Sister?'

'Alright. Alright. What do I know about it, I'm an old trumpet. What do I know about all your politics?' The other shrugged her shoulders. Kunigunda sulked, eyes cast down, her adored one had again ignored that look in which all was declared. Staring fixedly, her sullen countenance rested on her ample black convent apron, and the fingers of her hard masculine hands again grasped the beads of the rosary.

'That's why I've come to talk about things, dear Sister. The fact of the matter is that the money (our little Helen's) while we are talking about it, is not as indispensable to our Order (in today's circumstances) as we would like to believe. It would be good, very good, if we could further our aims with it. But in no way would it be suitable or even enough for us to give up all the plans we have for developing a sound financial base for the Order. You do follow me, don't you, gentle Sister?'

'Some higher kind of school,' grumbled Kunigunda. 'You all want higher education. In the Teacher Training School we've already got far too many difficult older girls, little madams training for marriage. One can't make them kneel or punish them, only be polite, it's a mercy we don't have to "ladyship" them. When it's their time of the month they turn quite green, and can hardly move themselves. What decadence. This boarding school in my day was a real education. Little ten-year-olds could knit stockings and embroider cross stitch, and there wasn't all this frilly fancy grading of study, elementary, secondary. Lucky they don't want a grammar school here. We certainly had order, that was for sure. None of them dared to whisper in front of me! Not like these experienced strumpets. Every month they go out to meals with relatives, I don't know where or with whom. And now we are to have a training college, whatever next!'

'In the old days', continued Virginia with enforced patience, 'we were sent more children of the Hungarian aristocracy to educate. Now we have become a boarding house, a cheap way of guarding adolescents. There is a reason for this, dear Sister. The demands of women's education are different now from thirty years ago. Also our detractors are criticising our old building as decrepit and unhealthy. Only last week one of the Jewish local papers had an article to that effect. Of course, we love our dear home, it's right for us. But to help our boarding school flourish again, and ward off ill will, we could do with some repairs to the cement pointing. Rising damp on the ground floor has reached waist level. The local authority wants to forbid us from burying any more people in the crypt. They say it's full and unhealthy.'

'So they want to dig out our dust from the earth, and disturb the coffins of our blessed departed!'

'No, no, they won't disturb them. And if they should place us, when the time comes with Christ's mercy, in the town cemetery? That is sanctified ground too. The angel's clarion call will sound there too, and gather us; amen. Our earthly lives were given us to toil for our salvation and receive rewards through suffering. Are we permitted deliberately to shorten our span?'

'Surely not!'

'So it is our duty to avoid illness and preserve our earthly lives given by our Heavenly Father. I spoke with our doctor yesterday. He had been attending our dear Mother. He mentioned our two sick sisters, including the honourable Gregoria. He maintained she need not have contracted tuberculosis. She was strong and healthy and past her twenties. And we should not lose by death two or three of our novices each year. Our Order has spent a lot, training them all in vain. They cannot then work for us and for the Glory of God. The old building is to blame. The seed of the trouble lies there. I don't understand these things myself. The doctor is an experienced man, a devout Catholic, and takes such trouble with our poor dear Mother. But these problems can be prevented and shall be prevented. The building will be repaired. Our sick sisters will be sent to a sanatorium, because, for this disease, God has shown mankind no other medicine but his own clear sky, fresh air and sun.'

'Stuff and nonsense. After this, anyone who wants a bit of fun, or time off at a spa, need only complain a bit: it hurts me here, it hurts me there, I'm delicate. . . . Why was nothing ever wrong with us old ones? Only the other day we were talking with Sister Leona during *regracio.* How is it Sister Martha has lived to be a hundred? It's all stuff and nonsense, American ideas.'

'Certainly,' interrupted Virginia quickly, perhaps sensing some innuendo, 'let's not talk of that. My dear Sister, you have probably heard that our financial situation has been . . . well a bit complicated in the last few years. While his Grace the late bishop was our Visitor, he was already old and ill for a long time, and conditions became ever more difficult; inflation, inept or unconscientious managers. Our honoured Father Fénrich, our new Prelate in Charge, is pressing for change, and for a higher income. Of course, we all labour hard for the Greater Glory of God; but we are few for great needs. We have to pay for so much secular help from young women in our sister houses, especially in our schools as the government now insists we must employ suitably qualified people. That is why we need our own institute for teacher training; and, in particular, so that we won't have to send our younger sisters out into secular institutions, for such a bitter time of study as I had, and several of the others. Then we would derive income from the new Institute — worth as much as an estate! And many of our pupils would be glad to stay on if they could acquire higher qualifications. There is also the moral benefit of training future school mistresses in our spirit, taking them away from the evil influence of modern secular institutions. Of course, it is most desirable at the start that there should be more of us to give our services, more new nuns who come here with readiness and joy; and most especially from that social class which has intellectual abilities, some influence, experience, even more important than money. . . . We do not usually talk explicitly of these things, kind Sister, but I want to keep you in touch. We have to defend ourselves against our enemies, who are also the enemies of our Holy Church. In that article I mentioned to you they also stressed the lack of bathrooms in our convent, that our school is deficient in scientific apparatus and equipment; and that the education we offer is not patriotic, not Hungarian enough! And. . . oh you are not listening to me! Have I offended you in any way? Am I wrong?'

'Oh, what do you care about me, what do any of you care? What about us, poor, unschooled, simple people, from an older world, the real members of our Order who are still here? We have gone out of fashion now, Sister Virginia, I can see that clearly. What do you want of me? You take not the slightest bit of notice of my words, my feelings, the love of my heart means nothing to you, I have known that for a long time. You are ashamed to remember the times we spent together, because I'm not learned. That's alright, it doesn't matter, simple hearts are dear to God. God did not command us towards worldly studies, the enticement of the Devil as Sister Simonea rightly says. . . . What are you talking about to me? Why are you talking? You know very well I don't read worldly newspapers, written by Jews. I don't understand your words, *college, social class, intellectual ability, health measures, scientific apparatus,* my tongue trips up on them. The

Bishop speaks like that, it's his job; I came here to pray, live in poverty and submission; I do my job, keep order as best I can. I've opened my heart to one person, and have been deceived; I've seen that for a long time, now I've had the proof! You didn't talk to me in this way when we still understood each other. "Improvements", "Reforms", the new sister is behind all this, the news has reached me too. That American woman, the learned woman, whose probation time was shortened (that's a new custom too) from three years to six months. Because she comes from a great family (as if that mattered before God); because she has been across the Atlantic (as if decent people didn't stay at home in their own country); because she decided at the age of thirty-two to follow our Lord, she has brought Him a head stuffed with learning and who knows what sort of a heart! And now here. . . .'

'Dear Sister, this is enough,' the other burst out loudly. She jumped up from her place, raised her rather large but beautiful hand in a hurt and forbidding way in front of her. 'I'm going!' she panted, because the last words had hit a sore spot. 'Forgive me, honoured Sister, if my visit has disturbed your prayers, and even more if against my intention I have provoked the sin of anger. I meant it otherwise, honoured Sister. I won't be a burden to you again in a hurry! Forgive me, blessed be our Lord Jesus Christ.'

'For ever and ever — oh — where are you rushing off to? I didn't mean it like that, wait . . . oh!' She again changed her tone from loud indignation to helpless, abject, frightened pleading. She held her two imploring fat arms towards the departing figure who did not look back, but hurried, scuttled on, her white veil floating agitatedly, angrily behind her handsome head. She had already reached the wire fence where she acknowledged the curtsies of the pupils, but withdrew her white hand from those who tried to kiss it. Kunigunda went no further.

'Look, look,' Erzsi Király nudged Marika Pável, 'those two have had a fight! Hey, what'll come of that?'

Kunigunda turned on her heel like a spinning top. Her face, burning with anger and passion, flushed into a most unlikely dark purple.

'So, that's the way you treat me,' she muttered incoherently as she returned to her table. 'Never mind. So be it. But no, you shall see. I'll thwart you yet!'

She picked up a great bronze bell, with which she used to gather her little flock; she rang it and rang it and rang it till the clapper nearly fell out, and everyone who heard it was petrified with fright. She tolled and rang and made such a noise without any break for so long that insects in the garden awoke, all those soporific beetles by the statue of the Madonna of Lourdes. *Has someone gone mad?* Along the wire fence the little girls had already been in their pairs for a long time in complete silence, standing stock still, scared, ready to go in for the luke-warm supper, and still she was ringing that poor bell. In between she shouted, shook her head stamped her feet, driven by embittered, despised passion, pathetic remnants of feelings repressed for so long.

'You useless bits of rubbish, you trash, what have I said, are you dumb? You'll open your ears.' And no one had the courage to smile.

FIVE

When she reached the cabbage beds Virginia slowed down and bowed in reverential greeting to old Father Szelényi who was taking his constitutional, clad in his greasy gown with an ageing umbrella under his arm. The priest took off his old wide-brimmed hat; and his face, which was like that of a genial ancient cook, smiled at the nun.

'Sister Virginia, you don't know our news yet? Our Rumkorff machine has arrived.'

'Is that so Father? I am truly delighted,' she replied also smiling. All trace of agitation had disappeared. Her voice and mien were again mild, courteous and calm.

'Come with me to the garden classroom; then I can show you straight away. You'll be amazed by the crackling, twisted lightning I can coax from it!'

'What sort of things?'

'Oh quite extraordinary! Crooked, curling heavenly miracles. It is such a clever machine.'

'Indeed.'

They laughed. The nuns were used to Father Szelényi, who liked to joke with them. They were aware that his exemplary life was well known to all priests of the diocese.

'You will be impressed when you see it, my dear Sister, and help me to get the X-ray machine I've been wanting these last six months. Will you come?'

'Tomorrow, dear Father, tomorrow in the morning I will look in on you in the physics lab for a few minutes. I am very busy just now.'

'Go on then, you poor historian! It's true that women and science don't . . . never mind. Bring Sister Magdolna with you tomorrow. We will test her and see what a foreign doctorate is worth.'

'Oh please do not mention that to her, dear Father!' Her face looked more lively for a moment. 'Sister Magdolna only desires to be thought of as a nun here, and nothing else. She gets upset by all reference to her former life. I've noticed, although she is so sensitive she never mentions this. She is truly remarkable, there is no pride in her.'

'Of course, a phenomenon, an angel on earth, a heroine. I know, I know. Aha!'

'I must go, really. May you be blessed.'

Her lively face calmed down quickly. She proceeded quietly along the kitchen garden, and the large bone beads of her rosary rustled gently in the folds of her dress. She turned her face towards the setting sun. She loved to feel the rays of the autumn sun on her half-closed eyes. She was enjoying it, but quickly disciplined herself remembering her training: *How great are the works of the Creator.* Without this the gentle pleasure of her skin would be sinful. On the right-hand side, in the garden of the novitiates, girls in their abigail dresses were walking under the trees. They were called into pairs under the fence by Berchtolda, in her motherly fashion; the nuns greeted each other from afar. The Mistress of the Novitiates cupped her hands and called out.

'How is Reverend Mother?' Her kindly concern rang across the garden.

'No change. Her temperature went up this afternoon. Pray for her.'

'We will, we will!' the young voices rang back reassuringly. Their white hands made the Sign of the Cross in front of their pale faces.

Virginia went on. In front of the gardener's cottage stood a little three-year-old toddler. His shirt hung out at the back. He glanced with indifference at the nun and continued to munch his brown bread. From birth he had been used to these women in black.

The garden path led out between flower beds through a vaulted gateway. The large leaved tree (even the gardener did not know its name) had already shed its fruit, strange, grey, hard and egg shaped. The novitiates made rosaries from these to be distributed among the poor women and pious 'congregants'.

On one side of a spacious courtyard where young acacias grew, the wide gate was open for the return of the convent's cattle herd. Heavy beasts, hardly able to manage their full udders, trudged slowly past the nun towards cowsheds further on. She got out of their way and turned her face aside. She felt a strange unease being near this group of animals, smelling of manure and weighed down by the burden of their female fertility. She remembered with antipathy a biology textbook, which discussed this useful domestic animal from the point of view of its economic potential.

She went through the farm gateway, by the drinking well and turned left. There a wide yellow single storey building had the following inscription above its old pillars:

SAINT JOSEPH'S HOSTEL
FOR UNFORTUNATE AND DISABLED CATHOLICS

By the entrance a nun was slouched in a wicker chair. Her wrists rested on her knees, both hands hung down uselessly thin and yellow like a skeleton. Her parched face was covered in tiny warts, its skin slightly puffed, the colour of faded ivory. Yet there was something childlike in this impossibly old face, its sightless eyes, stiff stare, and the rhythmic nodding of the waxen little head. She sat musing like this for the whole day. She was over a hundred years old. She was excused every fast, spiritual exercise, penance, no longer had to kneel on the stone floor or recite her rosary. Sister Martha could no longer sin on earth.

'Blessings on you! How are you, dear Sister?' Virginia stepped between the drinking troughs, to come up to her. The white veiled mummy face had not moved. Her impaired senses had not yet registered the voice or the approaching person.

'How are you?' Virginia asked her again. Then the old nun looked up with her sunken cheeks, sightless eyes, and she smiled.

'Very well,' she replied in German. Her voice was surprisingly clear. 'God's grace has not left me, a humble servant of God. The sun is shining on me.'

'Do you still like to live, Sister Martha?' (It was the custom in the convent, no one knew since when, to ask such a question from this hundred-year-old virgin bride of our Lord. And they knew the answer was always the same.)

'Oh yes, of course, as long as God permits.'

'Do you not long for your reward, the company of

saints? Do you not desire to see God face to face?'

'Oh no, not yet!' and the little wax face nodded faster. 'Why hurry?' she murmured. 'What is all the hurry? Eternity lasts for eternity. . . .'

That was what was left after the many thousand masses, fasting days, prayers, that was it, in the hundred-year-old soul: *Eternity lasts for eternity. Why hurry? The sun is still shining.*

The visitor made her farewells. With slightly bowed head and deep in thought, she continued her stately walk. She found herself in the courtyard of the school. From here the beautiful modern building with large windows was almost kneeling among the flower beds; cheerful with wide-open corridors and properly clean. The sister regarded it with pleasure. This was perhaps what she liked best. Recent and effective work, the open and unashamed quest for knowledge, and this dear house which was partly her achievement. It can't be a sin, to be attracted by worldly things . . . no, since the Lord of Hell is called Prince of Darkness; and Sister Martha who is a saint, like a young child, loves the sunlight.

She was a little confused nevertheless; searching for religious formulas, legal phrases, as ever, to apply to herself. She had reached the front of the great house. In the further courtyard of the double U-shaped building, the inhabitants of the left wing were sitting together under a great chestnut tree, praying and chatting; perhaps they were gathering for the Angelus, the evening bell. Virginia recognized strict Leona, gracious Simonea and Evelina the 'saint', who was still in her prime but had aged out of self-neglect, fasting and sleeplessness. Virginia bowed deeply from the waist towards them, and they replied in turn. Virginia then entered the other courtyard containing the main well and pump. The ground floor of the kitchen, refectory and church opened on to it. A smell of incense and caraway soup was all pervasive. Entering the cool corridor she experienced a very physical feeling and realized she was hungry. She had done some book-keeping work, and missed her tea. Her bread and butter would be there untouched at her place in the nuns' dining room. She could run in and eat it. Supper wouldn't be until half past eight. . . . But she did not go in. One must not neglect such small self-denials, useful for the soul, more useful sometimes than larger denials which often made one ill-tempered. She felt her stomach's needs with unusual intensity, considering her age. (Such things became important in their lives. They spent so much time in spiritual reflection that temptation of the senses included resisting hunger.) Turning into the corridor she almost fainted.

From the nursery, little children of the town were crowding out, through the gateway known as the 'porta', a noisy little army of tiny boys and girls. Sister Adele's strong refined voice could be heard in accelerating bursts as she led them. One small boy slept in her arms, his curly head pressed against her bosom; another ragamuffin was pulling at the folds of her apron. Adele was unchanged, still the same confident daughter of a Lord Lieutenant, Virginia reflected. She has been with us for ten years and there could be no serious complaint against her, and yet she has not assumed convent deportment or mannerisms. Adele walked out of the gate with the little ones, following them with her eyes for a while. Anyone might see her during this time — that couldn't be right! The student nurses were there. Such behaviour could cause critical comment among secular people. One had to take care about appearance, if one wished to influence the outside world and help its spiritual welfare. And what was all that commotion about at the bottom of the steps? Of course, Gregoria talking with the Very Reverend Father Fénrich. He had been working on the accounts in the study next to the porta. It was dusk now, time he went home. True, he and Gregoria were cousins and it would be a sin to doubt their Catholic relationship — but the sister was taking it to excess and might catch a cold by the open door. Perhaps she should be talked to, perhaps that would be a duty. How could one's conscience know at such times whether the motive was love, or jealousy? Might it be ill will? Oh dear!

The most clear-headed among them were sometimes beset by such small doubts. I must go to chapel, she said to herself. And as she touched her forehead with Holy Water by the entrance, all sense of hunger and physical discomfort seemed to disappear. Taking this as a good sign from her guardian angel, she knelt down by the first altar, the Grieving Mother, and hid her face in her hands resting on the prayer stool. The chapel was empty and silent. For her spiritual exercise she rapidly recalled her last hour, in case she had sinned. She had behaved proudly with poor old Kunigunda, yes she had lacked humility and sisterly compassion. What if she herself were to be dealt with in this way by the person whose approval and love she longed for? And had she not in her thoughts been censorious towards Gregoria for talking to Fénrich? When only a few minutes earlier she herself had been joking with Father Szelényi? Before confession on Saturday she would have to ask forgiveness from all her companions. She would make her peace with Kunigunda in the usual way, kissing on the left and right side but hardly touching. Does anything ever change with her?

She had surely lost the Old One's support for the causes she had tried to explain. But there were people who valued Kunigunda's opinion, particularly in the sister houses. They liked her frank speech, common sense: her peasant sayings travelled by word of mouth. But she must give her up now. Nobody would be able to pacify Kunigunda; ugly sinful jealousy had been awakened in her. 'The American sister'. . . those words had set Virginia off, made her angry, caused her to leave in indignation. Oh, but God can surely see how different was her pure friendship with that excellent, dear person. . . . Her spiritual admiration for this outstanding woman was so different from these awkward attachments, shady twisted feelings, secret tendencies! It was impossible that God should not be pleased, as she only wished to be a better person through Him and for the sake of Magdolna. 'God is surely understanding. I can only think of Him as some eternal strong *essence* which spreads freely and without end round every being.' Magdolna had said this the other day. She had lived her youth in the storm of life, had seen everything, knew everything, could think calmly without worry.

Magdolna did not close her eyes during the devotion of prayer, nor look upwards. Her wise countenance gazed steadily ahead during mass, and she sat with her hands resting in her lap, only kneeling down for ceremonies at the altar. What a fine, aristocratic soul this woman had. What a simple, wise personality; how steadfastly *holy*! It could only be a path to perfection — to take her as an example. But perhaps she was too preoccupied with her for God's will? Was it permitted to think in this way towards an earthly person, born in original sin? Was it not already *pride* to raise one's own feelings so high above others? 'Oh Lord lead us not into temptation; but deliver us. . . .' Yes; if her spiritual life were as calm and sure as that of Magdolna. If only she had seen the real world too, with *real* sin and *real* temptations! Oh these vicissitudes, these twisted thoughts. Perhaps they are the trials God sends for his chosen, to test them according to Thomas à Kempis. . . . 'Unworthy worries,' Magdolna used to say, 'they tire you unnecessarily and do not bring you nearer to your goal.'

Outside she could hear the faint bell calling to the *Ave*; and she had forgotten to pray here, in this sacred place. Virginia clutched her hands together with great will power, raised the whites of her eyes in the customary exalted expression, then slowly half lowered her thick lashes just as she had seen everyone else do — bar one. 'The angel of the Lord greeted Mary: she would conceive in her womb by the Holy Spirit. . .', she whispered.

SIX

In the senior girls' Dormitory Two (the small dorm), a night light was already burning on top of the tiled stove; it must have been just after nine o'clock. In breathless silence about a dozen girls lay on their narrow iron beds until, outside, the Old One's angry footsteps receded. She had blown herself out like a storm, and gone to have some rest. Geralda, her poor frightened deputy for the novitiates, was in charge. This silly kind creature was friend rather than prefect to the boarders.

'Little Sister,' Erzsi Király, leaning up on her elbows from the bed by the door, whispered towards her, 'don't worry! You can't take that kind of scolding seriously?'

'But why do you young ladies behave so badly? You know how strict Mother Kunigunda is; and it's very hard for me. You all just laugh.'

Marika Pável sat up in her bed and had such a fit of giggles, it spread to the others.

'Dear Sister,' continued Erzsi, 'you surely have sympathy for the soul's need to dream, haven't you? The full moon is so beautiful outside and so romantic; Cornelia imagined two large dark eyes and a passionate red mouth out there; she wanted to gaze at it from her own bed through the window, such shameless courage! She dared to put her own pillow at the *other* end of her bed and turned so that the moon shone into her eyes. You must have some poetic understanding for her?'

'Well, well I might, but you know Mother Kunigunda. And it isn't quite right when everybody's pillow is on the right side that one girl alone, without any authority, should put hers onto the left. You all just laugh!'

Marika could not control her laughter. 'This stinking moon,' she mimicked Old Kunigunda. 'What's gotten into you, you idiot? These crazy senior girls should be taken by the cuckoos!'

She did such a splendid impersonation of the Old One's voice and pronunciation that even sad Helen Gross smiled in her corner.

'You romantic girls read cheap novels about moonlight. You read such a lot of trash. It would be better for you to think about your spiritual welfare.'

'Have you never read a romantic novel?'

'I don't want to be untruthful. Once four years ago I did.'

'When you were still at home in Budapest with your parents?'

'Yes, a young gentleman who was my sister's lodger gave it to me. It was called *Sara* by George Ohnet. For all the world I would not want to read another. I could not sleep for a whole week it disturbed me so.'

'Oh goodness! What a successful writer this Ohnet must be. But I hope it doesn't disturb your dreams now?'

'No Erzsi dear, Mother Simonea, bless her for it, knocked that kind of nonsense out of us during our three years with her.'

'Yes, the novices could not live the jolly lives then as they can now with gentle Berchtolda.'

'Oh that was a different time; Mother Berchtolda is too lenient, that's certain. This is not true convent education. She encourages you to look happy and won't tolerate downcast eyes. She does not punish loud chatter or giggling, only admonishes gently: "Now, now, girls!" What kind of nuns will these become?'

'True, but this autumn so many candidates entered this convent, more than ninety of them, there have never been so many. We hear the Order needs more nuns, then secular teachers will no longer be required. They want to increase numbers. I've heard that the Kolba girl is going to enter, the one who lost her fiancé.'

'What's the use of having so many novices when they only bring in chaos from outside? No good will come of it. After a few years they leave, even though they have taken their vows, received their rosaries and the badge of the Order. God forbid they should become heretics. No priest at confession would absolve them for breaking their vows. We had a case like that ten years ago. I fear we shall get more soon.'

'Oh yes, a Protestant head teacher helped one of the nuns escape and he married her. But you know Sister, out in the world the prospects for marriage are getting worse each year, the value of girls is going down. That's why the convent is receiving so many applicants. It's becoming fashionable again to be a nun. If you manage, with difficulty, to find a commonplace water engineer to marry, he dies on you before the wedding.'

'Oh, Miss Erzsi, what things you say! I believe dear Jesus needs whole hearts, not broken ones. It is strange they allow her to keep the picture of her departed fiancé in her cell. We were trained differently and I preferred it.'

'It is strange the way our friends in the Training College, the youngest sisters, speak like this and are most strongly opposed to the reforms of Virginia and Berchtolda.'

'We remember best all the discipline and the reasons for it. We won't succumb to the first temptation life offers. Oh goodness me, in my time! Every term we held a ceremony, Asking for the Veil. We knew whose turn it was and when. This was only for practice, for self-denial and patience. In those days no one could take the veil in less than three probationary years, a time for suffering and humility. "You, you presume to take the veil. . . . You can't even open your mouth. . . . You would defile that sacred garment with your body. . . . Such a lewd creature wear the bridal garment of our Lord?" And so on for half an hour and then again after another three months. This custom has been dropped by Berchtolda. Just think. Boarders now enter the novitiate because life is more pleasant, less strict. That can't be right. We won't get such nuns as we used to get from this lot. You won't find the equal of Sister Evelina, a saint of fasting and self-denial.'

'Tell us, dear Sister, how you decided as a young girl from Budapest to become a nun. Was your heart whole?'

'What do you mean? I always went to the nuns for my schooling. When my parents went to the theatre with my sister, I chose to stay at home. I'd go to the kitchen and teach hymns to our servant. God helped me realize my calling from the age of ten. What a lot of unnecessary things we have talked about tonight, a waste of time. I'm going to my cell; three tenths of my rosary remain.'

'Please wait a moment. I must see you. Please!' A child's chilling voice could be heard from the doorway.

'Look at that!' said Marika Pável, twisting her fringe into the curling iron so that her hair will hang well in the morning. A spindly sharp-faced child entered from the corridor. Below her bright eyes and long plaited hair, two thin arms were crossed over undeveloped breasts. She looked with longing at the little nun. This foolish girl had crossed from Dormitory One, where Kunigunda herself was the superintendent. Kunigunda's cell opened into that dorm.

'Please, please!' she implored, while the older girls watched with amusement.

'Why do you do such mad things, getting yourself into trouble? You must stay in your proper place,' was the reply in a voice which controlled pent-up emotions.

'I couldn't bear it any longer. Please help me!' She was crying, desperate, her thin figure shivering in the white night-dress. She knelt at the chair near Erzsi Király's bed, hid her face in her hands.

'You must struggle. You must suffer.' The little girl choked with sobbing, her shoulders shaking.

'I can't. You must visit me sometimes,' she moaned. Geralda stood like a holy statue above the kneeling figure.

'Our Lord Jesus suffered for us on the cross. That is our duty too.'

This seemed to have an effect on the child. Her plait twisted like a snake down her back during her convulsive crying; she clicked her thin fingers, suffering deeply. Erzsi Király leaned down and pulled her hair.

'Listen Militoritz,' she laughed in irritation. 'Listen to me you crazy animal; stop moaning, or I'll give you such a slap you'll remember it on your wedding day. This nonsense is unworthy of you. I thought better of you. If that young sister had more sense (she's gone in now) she would knock the stuffing out of you instead of encouraging your silliness. She talks of suffering and passions to a monkey like you. All I've got to say is that, if you don't stop this tonight, I'll tell the Old One! Only a month ago in August you were writing letters to a charming friend in Debrecen, called Paul Ördög; but the letter was addressed to Paula Ördög, and instead of lots of love you signed with best wishes. You put it on Kunigunda's table, with all the other open letters, and the Old One sealed them. (Don't be frightened, it doesn't matter, other people hearing, we all write letters.) You had some courage then, before conforming to the ways of the convent. All fired up about a nun ... aren't you ashamed? She is a pathetic female like you are; how can you worship her? Get back to your bed, before the Old One comes back; you can take my shawl. Your cold will get worse in these icy corridors. Off you go! If you want to write to that Paul of yours again you can depend on me. We have a reliable daily from the village and she takes our letters too. How old are you? Fifteen? At the end of the year I shall write to your mother, though I don't know her, and suggest they find you a husband as soon as possible. Your family has money. Otherwise you'll be in trouble. NOW GOODBYE!'

'You've brought her down to size!' Marika was still giggling, having finished doing her hair at last, she plumped her pillow and turned to the wall.

Others were asleep or pretended to be. Szidu and Gidu were spreading out cards by moonlight, to find out whether they would be seeing the beautiful Emerika next day.

Erzsi could have shown a bit more understanding, thought Gidu, but she did not dare to say it out loud.

Two third-year enthusiasts were swotting up their chemistry standing on the chair by the stove to get close to the oil lamp. Another third-year girl with a pencil was preparing an essay for their Debating Society. She hoped to become president of the group next year. In the corner Cornelia and Helen were whispering. Their beds were next to each other and they leaned across heads almost touching.

'You love him don't you?' Erzsi could hear Cornelia speaking German in her strange Romanian accent. 'His name is Toffler, Albert, isn't it? He teaches at the grammar school in town. But is it the Catholic school? And you met him at Mrs Holzer's. Is he handsome, clever? Does he love you?'

'How can I know? He is my dream, that's all.'

'Do you think he loves you? One can usually tell can't one? You don't really want to become a nun do you? Reverend Mother would never force you would she? You don't look the sort. What would she say?'

'Oh I don't know; he probably doesn't think anything of me, I'm so ignorant and he is so clever, such a serious man. Er ist nur mein Ideal.'

Erzsi had been listening. She put on her petticoat and slippers and went over to them. Settling down as the third person on Helen's bed, she began her lecture about life and love.

She intended to write a letter to her special friend later that night.

SEVEN

On a misty autumnal morning, by the open corridors of the new building jutting out into the garden, Virginia and Magdolna were leaning against the carved wooden pillars. Huddled up in their black cloaks they looked out onto the frosted flower-beds and trees covered in white rime.

'Surely you agree with me?' asked the Italian woman, her eyebrows furrowed. She talked softly enjoying the intimacy. In the classrooms behind them, heating was already turned on and lessons in progress. The future primary-school teachers were studying teaching method, art and physics.

'Of course I do,' replied the other and turned towards her. White teeth flashed a delightful smile. There was something kindly and elegant in the slightly ageing face. Anyone studying her carefully would discover the reason. The traces of sexuality, of animated flirtation, had been erased from her features. One could seldom come upon simpler manners. The strange peace of her personality struck all who saw or spoke with her. The whole convent felt this special quality, without understanding it. She herself did not exploit this power, seemed rather to be unaware of it. Her fellow nuns wore the same habit, ate at the same table, though she differed from them in her origins, upbringing and experience.

'I agree with you entirely,' she repeated thoughtfully. 'But it doesn't seem so important.'

'You live here among us, Magdolna,' the other continued in her lively way. 'You chose our Order. (I know you preferred a working Order, and chose us.) We struggle for our salvation, for the salvation of others. We do not spend our lives only in divine worship because our poor souls are not fit for pure grace. I know it was Mary who chose the better half and not Martha. Here we are only Marthas.'

'Yes we should labour. But does it really matter what the circumstances are, who is our head, or any of these things? Our life will pass.'

'You must not talk like that. Perhaps you bring with you some slight disillusion from your former experience? That must not be. You have never told us in detail the circumstances which brought you here. It does not matter, of course. God chooses his own, as He did the twelve by the Jordan: *Leave your boats and follow me.* He draws souls towards Him by force or whatever means are necessary. And if you were chosen for this. . . .'

'I think you are right, my dear. I probably didn't come with a sufficiently willing soul. You were all young, in full possession of your qualities. . . .'

'Stop, don't say that. You are the dearest before God and all of us,' interrupted Virginia with such vehemence that she flushed. 'You have brought to us so much wisdom and learning. You have such eloquence, so many abilities. It would be impossible to consider a higher training college without you. You work so hard, you are our pride, truly.'

'Oh no, no!' Magdolna smiled gently, arresting and calming the passionate outburst. She had a delightfully modulated tone of voice full of humour and captivating kindness. 'You see,' she continued more sombrely, 'I do know you are right. One has to live the details, the tasks and preoccupations of daily life, with more humility, or there is the danger of self-pity. There has to be an underlying philosophy of life but at the same time one must not neglect or judge harshly the quiet mundane tasks. You are certainly right. We should not merely rise each day, eat and pray. So, please allot more work to me. Would you like me to write the letter which must be drafted to our sister houses?'

'Oh no! There is no need for that. You teach so many hours as it is. I will get Berchtolda to do that. Only. . . .'

'Well?'

'Do support us in everything. Be with us for the good of our Order. Don't oppose us if in this spirit we expect something of you. Something for which you are the most suited.'

'How could I oppose you!' Magdolna replied with unsuspecting simplicity and took her young friend's hand.

Virginia had meant to say something more but was paralyzed by this unaccustomed trusting physical contact. Her face flushed to the roots of her hair, she looked confused. On the dark cloth her hand lay completely still, her whole body deeply respectful — as during a religious ceremony in front of Holiness.

Magdolna's face became serious, and she withdrew her hand.

'We must hurry to our lessons,' she said as she

turned away. 'We've missed a quarter of an hour. I hope you haven't caught cold out here?'

Virginia did not listen to the question. As they walked on she hurriedly, passionately repeated her urging.

'You will agree with us, whatever we decide for you, won't you?'

Her nervous mouth twitched into a strange devoted smile.

'Well, of course my dear. The task you give me is too easy.'

'May God be with us in our tasks.'

'Amen. I have left a book in the staff room, the Academy publication of Ehrenfeld's codex. Oh don't rush off to fetch it for me. You put me to shame . . . . Really Virginia you shouldn't have done that.'

Virginia, still panting from her sprint, handed the heavy tome to Magdolna, with that same arch smile. Then they parted and went to their lessons.

As they passed the fourth-year classroom, Marika Pável nudged her neighbour Szidi.

'Look, those two have been larking around again instead of teaching. Did you see Virginia, leaping like a young deer?'

'Oh yes, my darling is in a great stew.'

'About what?'

'Well, don't you know? She wants to get her idol elected as the new Reverend Mother.'

'*NO* honestly, what an idea.'

'Haven't you heard? The whole convent is talking about it.'

Everyone seemed to know — except the person involved.

Erzsi Király, who sat behind Marika, carefully bent forward to hear what was said. These three heads so close together caught the attention of their religious instructor. Father Jóska Fóth stopped in the middle of a sentence, and looked at them severely. In spite of an attempted smile, his fat cheeks merely produced a kind of snout. Marika shut her pretty mouth, shrugged her shoulders like a housemaid (where could she have picked that up?) and looked away. She was 'cross' with the master — for some reason. Szidi cast her eyes down quickly. Erzsi on sudden impulse leant back on the bench and dreamily, carelessly returned his stare. She amused herself to the end of the lesson, testing the vanity of this handsome man. Next she rested her chin on her hands, elbows in lap, and looked upwards with wide eyes returning his gaze for several seconds. After that she pretended to be absorbed by something behind her. As soon as she felt his stare she shuddered, turned forward and managed to blush like a practised actress. Finally, when Father Fóth was trying to explain a complex theological point concerning the fate of the souls of unbaptised infants, Erzsi decided to embarrass and entangle him again. She succeeded. Then, luckily, the bell went for the next lesson. But did Marika notice these games?

Out in the corridor after the lesson Erzsi met her maid from the town, a Jewish girl. From apron to apron something was carefully transferred: a letter in a large white envelope addressed in neat writing. In the same way, with magic speed it was slipped into the blue-paper cover of her physics workbook. It could only be read at night, when everything was quiet in the dormitory, leaning against the stove to catch a gleam from the oil lamp.

'Are you worried?' Gidu teased poor Cornelia before Kapossy's German lesson.

Marika was adjusting her hair with the aid of a little hand mirror. She then examined the reflection of her figure in an empty glass case, tied her apron stylishly and went out. What's this? Is she going out to speak to Kapossy before the lesson? What can that mean? A moment later they could see her through the window standing by the German teacher, explaining something. She was shrugging her shoulders, playing with her apron-strings, biting her red lips, smiling awkwardly.

'Look at that idiot. She's gone to confess she hasn't done her homework. What's come over her? I saw her doing it, studying the boring life of Klopstock. . . .'

'Making such a fuss about easy homework!' One of the town girls was shocked.

'What must the teacher think of our class?'

'Look, look how Kapossy himself is blushing!'

Cornelia Popescu, suffering in silence, had leant forward to get a better look at them. Her hands hung down in her lap; her dark eyes were fixed in astonishment.

'He's talking with her, how awful! Explaining things, asking her questions, worrying about her. Can't he see she is only preening herself? Exaggerating now, like a peasant girl. Why can't she be satisfied with that fool Fóth?'

'Look my little Fata, look dear wife,' Erzsi smiled, standing by the window. Although it was a German lesson she still clung to her blue-paper covered physics notebook. Outside Kapossy was gathering his robe round his knees, like in pictures of saints, and let Marika walk on his right side. They entered the classroom together. Cornelia cast down her eyes: her face expressed sullen indifference, her posture slumped — neglected. She did not care about anything, as long as she could continue to dream. Erzsi was observing Marika, who sat through the lesson profoundly absorbed, as never before, listening to the teacher with deep attention. Her whole behaviour was exemplary. Erzsi decided to try an experiment. Could she open her letter without being observed? She rustled and fussed in the silence. But, for the last ten minutes, as some poor girl had been stumbling and hesitating over her translation, Erzsi, who had only got to the outside of her large white envelope full of small neat letters, was called on to assist. She extricated herself with difficulty. Thankfully her German was good.

'Today is "male" morning,' said Marika, who always tried to be witty, relieved from her efforts of false attention. She laughed a lot in the corridor as they proceeded to the science lab. The reference was to Tuesdays when for three consecutive lessons she could breathe the same air as male teachers.

They had a long wait for Father Szelényi. Usually he smoked his cigar for half an hour in the staff room, chatting to some nun who happened to have a free period. The fourth-year girls were quite noisy before their physics lessons, knowing Father Szelényi was not disturbed by that. He used to say: 'Silence is not necessarily more righteous than noise! Some sins are committed in deep silence; theft for example. On the other hand the sacred synod, debating the fate of your immortal souls against those of the unbelievers, cannot pronounce a verdict in total silence. Do not misunderstand me, young ladies. No one doubts your possession of tongues.' He talked such nonsense; expression innocent, eyes mocking from the frame of flesh called a face. If some clever artist, or a concave mirror, faithfully reproduced his head, one would see a bald cherub with a broad-brimmed greasy hat; food stained clerical garb, and the inevitable fat cigar; that was how he entered now, Diogenes dressed as a priest, the beloved sage. He walked cheerfully between the tall glass cases with their flesh-coloured casts of human limbs, model machinery, glass tubes and flasks. Silence fell as he sat at the head of the table looking mischievous. Slowly, oh so slowly, he rummaged for his notes and tension mounted in the class (unforgettable games of 'danger'!). The buzz of a lone fly was audible, trapped in the intricacies of a biology model of the human ear. Slowly and even slower than that, Father Szelényi pulled the little pencil from his notebook. The whole class, boarders, day girls and novice nuns, held their breath. Painfully he opened his notebook, looked among the names with an executioner's calm, and at long last called up one of the nuns. Deep sigh of relief all round.... These novices might be stupid but they did not come unprepared and Father Szelényi does not expect too much knowledge of science from women. Marika was asked next, and performed quite respectably.

He praised her rather daringly. 'So, so you have special knowledge of the science of hair curling!' He knew about her behaviour in the German class.

'He can see right through people,' whispered Szidu, busy with Gidu decorating the biology model of the ear with bits and pieces to create a witty caricature. Nobody enjoyed a joke better than Father Szelényi.

What a lot went on during a long morning.

In the ten minute break, Marika stopped by the corridor railing, her face frosty with sarcasm.

'Congratulations!'

'Same to you,' Erzsi laughed back at her. They both knew what they were talking about, although neither had mentioned either Fóth or Kapossy. Erzsi, remembering Cornelia's feelings, thought: Take care, you vain toad!

The last lesson was drawing with the languid Gregoria, who was ill with TB. No more homework required. They took models out of the cupboard, plaster ornaments: a rose, a palm, a tulip, a lotus and an inanely large classical head of Juno. That all took time; the pale nun sat at her podium throughout the noise and drummed her blue-white fingers.

'Another loud word and I walk out': the fretful impatience of a sick person's weak voice; behind her face the stiff veil crackled. Soon the noise subsided. Novices in front turned round to quieten the day girls and boarders.

An occasional sound of pencil sharpening might be heard here and there. Gregoria received the drawings brought to her in silence, corrected and rubbed out in her apathetic way. Her white face expressed nothing, her eyes had deep rings round them — perhaps not only from the disease. Her thin mouth was feverish red, above a slightly sharp chin. What would her face have looked like in profile with an open forehead not covered in white headgear? Did that help to make her a picture of suffering, nourishing itself on yet more suffering, indifferent to everything else?

In the two back rows cautious conversations started up. Lips hardly moving, neighbours on the benches related whole stories to each other.

'Listen it's true, but don't tell anyone,' began a plain and poorly dressed little girl. 'You know I board with the mother of Father Fóth; and the same washerwoman goes to work for her and for old Mrs Fénrich, who is the grandmother of Sister Gregoria and Father Fénrich. She brought up both of them, as they were orphans, or their parents had gone to America. They are cousins you see, the washerwoman told me. I know she is old now, but she did do the washing there when those two were both little. She told their grandmother that the two children were always so quiet together and hiding away, it couldn't be right. Once, both of them were beaten severely for it, but later the washerwoman felt guilty about her criticism of them. She realized the little girl hadn't developed quite normally. She could never have had any children. It was best to send her to be a nun. God marked her in some way. I don't know what she meant, that's what she told me anyway. Who knows what truth there is in the gossip of an old drunken washerwoman. It might not be true. But don't tell anyone else and don't say I told you!'

'If you young ladies have important things to talk about, I would ask you to go out into the corridor and carry on there.' From the desk the drawing mistress gave her listless reprimand. She was so far from them, their talk, their lives, their preoccupations with growing up, only desiring silence, silence, for she could not bear anything else.

In the other corner there was more chatter, two senior girls whispering together. Loath to criticize them she turned her face away from twenty-two-year old Erzsi and Helen, niece of Reverend Mother. To keep Helen occupied she was made to take some kind of language course, for which drawing was a compulsory adjunct. She came down to join the fourth-year group for this.

'So, German girl, how often have you two talked together seriously?'

'Oh dear me, perhaps three and a half times. The fourth doesn't count because Mrs Holzer came in and disturbed us, just as it became interesting. Toffler had said that faithfulness is a German virtue.'

'Are you sure he meant faithfulness in Love?'

'I don't know, he is such a serious man. Perhaps he meant he'll always be faithful to his old fiancée. I heard about her from Mrs Holzer. They parted because the girl was not fit for him. A lousy Hungarian bitch — Oh don't take offence.'

'Since then you've not spoken to him alone?'

'No. Only that last time, three weeks ago, after our exeat, I came back at seven. He and the Holzers brought me back. She arranged for us to walk a bit ahead of them. Then he, Mr Toffler, said very quietly to me almost in my ear: "You have to go back into that ugly old house. It'll be such a long time before I can see you again." So I said to him: "Does that worry you?"'

'You little German, you certainly know what to say!'

'Oh Erzsi, he started saying something more. I think it was "Look my dear Helen", then he hesitated, and Mr Holzer, my friend's husband, called to us and we had to stop. They talked about boring things, rules for the matriculation exams, and about the director of the education committee, and by then we had reached the gates of the convent.'

' "We'll still be good friends, won't we?" was all he could say as we parted and he held my hand very tightly.'

'What more did you want?'

'But that's nothing. Why did he say "good friends"? He could have said something more, couldn't he? Or is that what he meant, that I mustn't expect more? He is too serious to flirt with a young girl. I think he still loves that silly Hungarian girl who dances and messes around with the officers, and has no character. Mrs Holzer told me that he caught her out just as they were about to get engaged. He loved her deeply. Oh dear, why do the best men waste their love on worthless girls? Oh Erzsi, nothing good can come of this. It's best if I become a nun. He's just my ideal man.'

'I would like to exchange a few words with that German gentleman!'

'For Heaven's sake!'

One of the candidates entered with great commotion and handed a sheet of paper to Gregoria, who glanced at it, turned even paler, dropped the note from her hand.

'Dear Helen,' she said as if she were suffocating. 'Go at once my angel!'

When Helen had left she got up, and looked stiffly across the class with those deep-ringed eyes.

'We must pray, we have had a death.' She spoke in a stifled tone and fell to her knees. Her rosary beads and the skull symbol of the Order clattered down with her.

EIGHT

For a whole day, from morning to night, the inhabitants of the ant heap lived underground. They knelt on the stones of the crypt, gazed into the flickering flame of the funereal light, fasted till they felt giddy, eyes glazed. A rhythm of deep prayer filled the stuffy, vaulted cellar. Some hundred pairs of lips chanted in turn, responding each to the other. Eternal recitative renewed a thousand times the dark murmur which died away and returned. Their heavy sense of pain gradually transformed, became as healing and peaceful as the thought of Eternity: *Grant us O Lord, eternal peace*. . . . From time to time exhausted younger pupils dozed off, the older ones let their imagination float upward, far away; towards noon, pale Janka Wester fainted, falling out of her prayer seat. One of the nuns, her relative, picked her up, took her out into sunlight, revived her. The nun then returned, nothing was allowed to disturb the service. For if the saintly departed had even unconsciously given space to a sinful desire during the short time between the raising of the blessed host and death of her mortal body; or delighted during her last moments in some vain pleasures of the flesh; or if she had the Evil Spirit lurking in her, causing her to regret the convent life of prayer and fasting (or even to doubt the approach of Everlasting Life and Truth) — and if for such a moment of error the penalty were a hundred years of Purgatory with wailing and gnashing of teeth in the terrible flames, her poor soul would yet have risen directly among the chosen Saints: because every prayer said for her was worth a hundred days of indulgence according to the official decree of the heir to St Peter, and the Eternal Judge would pardon her sinful soul for a full hundred days! O wonderful power of Faith!

After their holiday for the day of mourning, the schools opened again — the inhabitants of the house rose at half-past five as usual, when the early bell tolled. By six they had finished making beds and getting dressed; kneeling on the floor in their rooms, they recited morning prayers until half-past six, and then on through the morning Angelus; mass followed in the chapel, and at quarter-past seven acorn coffee with the morning's *silencium*, which was accompanied, of course, by prayers at the table and supplication for departed souls while walking along the corridors. Students went to their lessons before eight o'clock, most of them through the great courtyards to the school house in the garden. There the voice of Kunigunda could no longer follow the boarders, there they might see men as teachers, even though they were priests; and there, from their day-girl friends, they had confidential news of the town, events, gossip, theatre: of *life*. Lunch with prayers and the noontime Angelus followed lessons.

In the afternoon, there was needlework in the parlour, or homework, or music practice — piano or choir; tea with prayers during the repast; the same at supper, with the evening Angelus and a tenth of the rosary to do; and finally *regracio* and a half hour of kneeling for evening prayers, mutual searching of conscience to recall sins committed that day. On Sundays and Holy Days they also went to the afternoon service in the chapel and during the course of the morning attended a longer sung mass. It was recommended that before sleeping at night everyone should kneel and pray by her own bed as if at a prayer stool. . . .

So the days passed here as they had for innumerable years. If from time to time the individuals under stiffly starched veil or in the narrow student beds changed, what difference did that make? Reverend Mother's simple room stood empty, the little flock of our Lord had no shepherdess — for the time being, her absence was imperceptible. The Bishop of the diocese, a stout reptile-eyed old gentleman, who had inducted the departed Reverend Mother, merely ordered the nuns to keep the customary three months of mourning with three meatless days each week.

The nuns, therefore, frequently had fish stew for lunch and wore black aprons over the normal habit. And everything continued along its usual course.

Real winter was upon them. They heated the rooms and no longer took students down to their beautiful large garden. Kunigunda stormed and fumed, Gerolda complained morning till night. In the main building everyone continued performing their duties. The young postulants listened meekly to Berchtolda's maternal admonishments on love, perfection and holy poverty, they were well versed in her teaching; yet the noise of their whispering and youthful giggles along the dormitory corridor during the hour of *silencium* often shocked the older nuns. Berchtolda, newly in charge of the postulants, did not agree with outward symbols of convent behaviour such as downcast eyes. She praised the courageous open religious heart. Evelina, the 'saint of abstinence', continued to fast beyond the stipulated times, and rose secretly at night to scrub the cold stone corridors even though this was not her job; she then had to teach needlework by day in the elementary school with hands roughened by caustic soda.

In the nursery, next to the great gate, Adele continued to befriend her young 'male admirers', took them into her lap, pressed them close to her beautiful bosom — if a little sleepy head happened to nod off there — and chattered away cheerfully, maternally in her native Hungarian way. By the wide staircase one could see Gregoria together with Father Fénrich (Bursar and Chaplain) more often than was strictly necessary. He was a consecrated priest, member of the Church and cousin of the beautiful nun, so it would have been sinful to have any suspicions regarding the two of them. Yet nothing should be done to excess, and standing around in cold corridors was not sensible behaviour for a sick nun. Magdolna went about in her usual way, simple, kindly and a little apart, with her pleasant clear smile and aristocratic movements; she gave most interesting lectures to her classes, and was able to convey history with great insight and wisdom; and with instinctive tact she kept apart from the minor politics of the convent. Of course, she liked and appreciated her friend Virginia.

Sister Martha continued to sit as before, but in her room in the hospice — on the terrace the sun rarely shone. Her two waxen hands hung down; with her head she nodded 'yes' and her childlike countenance looked out into space. Father Szelényi messed around till evening in the physics laboratory and nagged Virginia to acquire the new X-ray apparatus; Kapossy caught up his cope like a gown, and pontificated, his sullen dark eyes throwing bolts of lightning against all enemies of the Church or morality. By Christmas he had reached *Sturm und Drang* in German and the followers of Rousseau in teaching methods. Father Fóth strode up and down the corridors with his mouth puckered, whistling. Cornelia Popescu dragged herself around with tired indifference, her dark eyes rarely lit up with any magic fire; Marika put her hair into cold-metal curlers every day; and Szidu and Gidu tirelessly pursued young Sister Emerika. . . .

And yet, perhaps all this was mere surface, these were not the significant happenings; anyone watching really carefully (maybe with God's gentle and all seeing eye) would notice other things. For example: Virginia and Berchtolda were often together in deep unison and seemed to find much joint 'official' business, they treated the ever unsuspecting Magdolna with affectionate humility in all matters, and found two of the Hungarian sisters to be on their side, lively Adele and pale Gregoria, beautiful cousin of the Bursar priest. The group of retired nuns met and talked together more than ever, during the evening *regracio* hour they were most frequently in dear Sister Simonea's room and usually Evelina, the saintly German girl, was with them; often they invited Kunigunda as well. Young Helen Gross in her mourning dress might also be worthy of observation; how many of the nuns, older and younger, hugged her to their hearts, though only gently in the permitted way, and kissed her twice on her face in the convent fashion saying, 'I would like to be a mother to you in the place of the departed; trust me dear child!'

Finally, it was noticeable how Cornelia Popescu and Marika Pável had not spoken to each other for some time; every evening Marika would praise Father Kapossy in a loud voice, saying how much wiser and better he was than, for example, Father Fóth who just happened to be handsome — so what? In a man that didn't mean much, he was conceited rather more than he was handsome; as for eyes, Kapossy's were striking. Erzsi Király, amused as usual, would quietly throw in a remark, 'Oh really?' or 'Is that so?' She was nodding her head from her standing position above the stove, which still retained some heat, where she leaned against the wall and busily scribbled something on torn out leaves of note paper.

Others walked around with mild reflective looks and nothing seemed strange to them. The old physics teacher, Father Szelényi, with his greasy gown and large cigar, was one of these. He loved everything about this little world — and therefore noticed everything which took place in the house, and in hearts and minds. Anyone he chanced to meet, he engaged in conversation.

'Aha — dear Sister Kunigunda you are not a friend of higher learning? "For such little monkeys" — there is some truth in that! You obviously believe in the sayings of the wise Romans: *The Elders should decide*. Sister Virginia is so interested in the emigration topic; she is interested in so many general topics, isn't she? Of course, only if they do not conflict with the duty of institutional charity. But she would surely like to know at what age, over there across the ocean, women have their political rights and whether in the hosiery factories the colour blue has eclipsed all the other colours of the rainbow? Has the health of my dear friend Gregoria improved at all? Will she be going to Switzerland this summer? I know what that will depend upon, perhaps she does too. Or perhaps she does not really want to go away from here? I have never seen a woman who understands so much *in theory* about economic management! Naturally, it indicates a family heredity of talents. The present fourth-year students? We have never had a more gifted class than this one. Some can no longer be treated as girls, but rather as mature women (which is why I call them wise Dianas); no, no I wasn't hinting at you two, Miss Szidonia and Miss Gizella, though I suspect you applied it to yourselves. Obviously it isn't a law of nature that fair hair always has to be long . . . how shall I put it? We will soon have to clarify the point; because not every nun of this Order has her natural head covering cut short when she takes the habit. Well we shall see: will we have the traditional performance of "shaming" before admittance to the Order? Aha!'

Thus he teased and joked in his simple foolish manner in the physics laboratory or staff room or in the corridor of the new building, always surrounded by an admiring public. He was a lonely old priest without family, living in a rented room on his small salary. He had no friends in town or at the Bishop's palace, he desired no advancement, never went out and, apart from the convent, met no other women. This was his 'natural science laboratory', his club and circle; mild banter was his social life.

Of those nuns who took an interest in Helen Gross, Berchtolda, Mistress of the Novitiates, won over her confidence the most. She was a decent and sensible woman — ugly and common, snub-nosed, with a squint, light blue eyes. She was the orphan of a local minor official and had started a sewing business with her aunt; she had delivered the finished goods. By the age of eleven, Berchtolda knew all that was going on, all the gossip and moral standards of the women of the town. Her aunt, an old maid, died unexpectedly; and this chaste, priggish little girl felt *a calling* towards convent life. With such precocity, desire for study and good judgement, she was sent for the diploma course. In the sister house she met Virginia, on whose recommendation the late Reverend Mother promoted Berchtolda to become Mistress of the Novitiates, replacing the ageing and ailing Sister Simonea who had not yet reached sixty, the retirement age. Berchtolda in her usual way spoke openly, maternally, frankly to the young Bavarian girl.

'How old are you, my dear?'

'I am twenty years old, dear Mother.'

'So until your twentieth year you lived out in the world. You are still uncertain about life and have not found the right way for yourself. Have you had suitors?'

'In Munich I never went to balls or out into company, my guardian did not want me to, because. . . .'

'Yes?'

'He wanted me to marry his cousin. But I didn't want to and told him I would rather come to my aunt and become a nun.'

'Is that how it was! We cannot become a Bride of Christ out of spite or childishness. Why did you oppose him? Was there someone else?'

'No — not at that time.'

'Not at that time? But since then? You can talk openly to me, as you would have done to your mother had you known her. I know worldly feelings prevail outside and do not judge you for that. Marriage is after all one of the Seven Sacraments. You do not have to give me names or particulars. Do you have thoughts and feelings for someone, a man?'

'Yes,' the German girl confessed in a quiet suffocating voice.

'So! And are your feelings reciprocated? Can you

expect what is called *earthly happiness*? Can you expect that from him? Well what do you think, my dear?'

Young Helen's brown eyes were covered in tears, her mouth trembled and she pulled out her handkerchief.

'No, no! He is just a dream for me.'

'Might you be mistaken? Are you sure your feelings are not shared?'

Helen bowed her head lower, and indicated yes in her handkerchief, or perhaps it was only a crying spasm. Tears dropped, like springtime thawing her young life as orphan and stranger. She was taking comfort in sentimental German lovesickness which she could only express in untranslatable words of poetry: *Wehmut, Demut, Schwermut.*

Her sorrow had been nourished by the visit of her kindly friend from the town, Mrs Holzer, who had wanted to show sympathy as soon as she was permitted, after a period of mourning, to come to the convent. Embracing Helen in the parlour she had blurted out some gossip and news from outside.

'Did you know that we are going to have an amateur performance here? I shall take part as it is for charity, Toffler has been asked too. I've heard that *that other girl* is also going to act. She came into town for carnival. They have given her a horrid part: she is supposed to be very beautiful and wicked, leading everyone astray. It's going to be very funny, those two performing together again!'

That had been all. Helen, of course, knew she would on no account be permitted by strict Kunigunda to go out visiting her friends at such a time, while still in mourning. For months or even longer she would be unable to see him whom she called *Mein Ideal* in her hot shy day-dreams. That thin link between them, of understanding glances and brief holding of hands, would be severed and disintegrate if there was no opportunity to strengthen their relationship. Oh she knew enough about men for that; and, moreover, the other girl would be there, they would meet, talk and resume their friendship. . . . Hopeless, fearful girlish pride and obstinate unhappiness — she bathed her pillow each night with tears and renounced life for herself. She didn't care about anything! As long as *he* would never know that a heart had broken for his sake.

'If it's like that my dear. . . ', Berchtolda stroked her brown hair. 'But don't cry, don't do that! These sorrows will pass I know. No feeble earthly man is worth it. . . . If matters are really thus, you are right in what you said before. Consider the matter carefully, many sad broken hearts have sought comfort within these walls.'

She nodded fussily — confident in her understanding and knowledge of worldly things — and held out her hand to be kissed. Helen was slightly comforted by the thought that she herself would *have to consider the matter carefully*; and enjoyed the role of tragic heroine in her own story. This was much more effective than when another nun, old Mother Leona, told her of her dream of the previous night in which the late Reverend Mother had appeared and expressed the wish that her niece should follow in her footsteps and enter her beloved Order.

'Are we doing the right thing and in the interest of our Order, dear Sister Berchtolda,' Virginia worried from time to time, 'by nursing this tendency in young Helen? You know our enemies could accuse us of having designs on her fortune, and. . . . Well, you know how some of our sisters behave who do not share our vision for the future of our Order. (May God in his infinite wisdom turn everything for the best!) We know how they think: "This dowry would get us out of our present serious difficulties, and we could put off our more fundamental improvements and repairs. Why bother with higher education, more helping hands, more extensive administration, when we can fix it all with cash, and everything can stay as it is?" I must confess I would be relieved if our Order no longer had to rely on dowries. Could we achieve that? True suitability, true vocation would be the criteria, no one would have to be persuaded — with better management and hard work that should be possible. You and I know that.'

'Yes we know it, dear Sister, and there are more of *us* than we thought,' nodded Berchtolda as if she knew more about the canvassing than anyone else. 'It's obvious when reading between the lines of the letters we are receiving from the Abbesses of our sister houses, and getting the gist of the mood out there. Oh you can rest assured, sweet Sister. It's quite clear that any money, from whatever source we receive it, will help our worthy aims rather than make them superfluous.'

'God be praised if it is so, dear Sister. Providence would appear to be on our side! I believe with all my heart in the goodness of our cause; though the Holy Spirit comes to all. I know the others mean well, but not by the right route in my opinion. May God protect me against error and evil. They clearly harbour resentment against us and are always in their own huddle.'

'That will disappear, dear Sister, dissolve as soon as our Heavenly Father has made known his choice in the election.'

'Just so, dear Sister, and our duty then will be humility and tolerance,' replied Virginia in earnest self-deception, and departed reassured by their mutual orthodox platitudes.

Christmas time came during the period of mourning,

and was monotonous with the usual succession of prayers and masses. Most boarders went home: during the holiday only Helen and Cornelia remained in Dormitory Two, day-dreaming (Cornelia had been invited home by her uncle but did not wish to go); and Marika, who kept setting her hair in curlers (she had written to her father, the station master, to ask for a gold watch for Christmas instead of money for the journey home). There was no New Year Dance either. In other years it was the custom for pupils, novices and postulants and even some of the nuns to congregate in the Nursery, as that was the largest room in the convent; someone would play the piano and then the dancing would begin. Some of the dance partners, beautiful young nuns, might be booked weeks ahead by adoring young pupils. For the slow csárdás they could only be asked on the night, when it was the custom to hesitate for a while and then, in priestly style, reluctantly make a few steps; while the *courtier girls* were busy performing, and dissolved in delight until the *organizer* shrieked out at them. Szidu and Gidu stayed behind every year just for that one evening during the Christmas holidays, but this year with sad hearts they wrote agreeing to go home; this year they could not dance with delightful Evelina.

After ten days they returned overfed, cheerful, in lace-sleeved new dresses. Erszi Király also wore a lovely new dark-grey gown; one could see what a fine full figure she had, and what snow-white healthy skin, what an elegant neck and shoulders; how glossy was her thick wavy hair dressed in the English style.

'Yes,' she whispered to Cornelia, who greedily examined her appearance down to every detail before Kunigunda commanded her to change into the blue convent uniform, 'on the very first day I got my dear mother to agree to have new dresses made for me.

(Luckily our dressmaker is a Jewish girl and the poor dear worked day and night.) On the third day of the holiday, my friend managed to get away from his affairs and came as he had promised. How marvellous and kind he was too! Such a man deserves every blessing. I tell you my other dress is even nicer, black velvet, cut deep at the front but with a white silk inset for more decorous occasions. I was able to show it to him for a moment in the changing room. For New Year we had an officers' evening (my brother organized it) and my friend was able to come to that as well; "The Member for our district who is with us in town," wrote the local paper. We were able to have fun together the whole evening. My mother is so sensible and understanding. And imagine, we travelled here together in a first class carriage.'

'Go downstairs, take off those clothes! Immediately. You shameless hussies. These brazen, horrible clothes.I don't want to see them for one moment longer!'

The Old One was herding, bullying them along to the changing room, to watch them take off their individual, comfortable, foreign, *untidy* home garments , they reminded her of the limits of her power.

In the middle of January, however, Erzsi Király was able to wear her beautiful black velvet dress; with, of course, the white silk inset for serious occasions. Sister Virginia wanted the St Teresa Circle of the student teachers to celebrate Founder's Day, as they did each year. The Training College was a separate institution, mourning in the convent did not affect them in the same way.

The girls filed class by class to the benches in the large hall, day girls in smart but cheap and badly-tailored dresses, just the occasional dazzling individual decoration showing their young charms. Blue-clad boarders whispered in groups and giggled quietly, postulants and the novices stood around the piano in suitable modesty. Here in public, correctness was the rule — only on their own in the novitiate did they dare to be cheeky. At last the room was quiet, they all stood up, the teachers filed in as one group: Kapossy as honorary Head was the leader, his puckered brow and splendid eyes sparkling as usual, as if on the defensive against some terrible insult. The religious instructor followed, Father Fóth, handsome, with his insolent rustic smile. Father Szelényi, as soon as the last chord of the anthem had died down, sat behind him, fat hands resting, looking deeply contemplative, for he had been obliged to leave his cigar in the corridor. He really could not smoke in here. Of the teaching nuns only Virginia, Magdolna and pale Gregoria, the drawing teacher broken in health, were present.

After the announcements an ambitious third-year student read her essay; a notable achievement, full of deep ideas. She had worked on it for twenty nights, forcing Erzsi off her place on the warm stove; adding half a page during each *regracio.*

She started to read in her high, festive, slightly choking voice reminiscent of a wailing woman:

> Man sets out on his terrestrial path. He hurries, presses forward, struggles breathlessly. His feet bleed from sharp stones, perspiration breaks from his brow, his bare head is pierced by the burning rays of the sun, but fainting he presses on, and with the last ounce of his strength goes towards his goal. At the side of the path tiny scented flowers smile at him, but no, he does not reach out to pluck them. His ardent eyes are fixed on their target, where in the heights the green palm flourishes. The end is far away, the high air is cold and

> foggy. But that does not worry the pilgrim! A vain worldly wish for praise is in his soul; he does not see the flowers opening, or feel the scorching heat of the sun; he rushes ahead, on and on . . . though his strength is failing, his blood is dripping turning the dust red . . . and so on, and on and on!

The young pioneer piped with intonation reminiscent of romantic recitals in village halls, until her stubborn symbol, Man, at last realizes that earthly struggles are in vain. In a collapse of exhaustion she finally enlightened her audience — Man found no peace for his soul because that 'dwells only in religion, by resting in God's divine providence'.

When the author, hoarse and flushed with effort, her forehead sweating, returned to her place, the girl who had the task of criticizing jumped up from her bench. She wore a red blouse and her hair was artificially curled.

'According to my humble opinion,' she read, a little confused, from a crumpled piece of paper, 'the talk we have just heard was written in excellent style, rich in language and in moral content. The introduction was particularly beautiful, although I felt it was a little long in relation to the rest of the argument. Her description of human suffering and disappointments was graphic, obviously arising from true experience. The conclusion was full of poetry but in my opinion she used the word "perspiration" too often. It could have been avoided, or some other word substituted. Furthermore, she wrote in one part that the "high air was cold and foggy" although in the previous sentence she had spoken of green palms, and we know that this southern plant will not grow in cold foggy places. We can learn this from our delicate house plants. (Uncalled for mirth — the girls remember Kunigunda's plant.) Apart from this, the writing of such a long essay shows great diligence, and is praiseworthy from someone in the third year, who in a year's time will be taking her final exam, the results of which will influence her whole life.'

'That criticism is on the whole justified,' nodded the imperturbable 'judge' Kapossy. 'I would just like to ask one thing: you criticized the use of the word perspiration. Can you tell us what you would have used instead?'

The little red-bloused girl blushed to the roots of her hair, stared stiffly ahead, looked helpless like someone waiting for prompting. 'Sweating,' 'flushing', etc., could be heard in the shocked quiet room, but she did not dare repeat any word.

'All right then,' the Headmaster finally said with his dry smile, realizing he himself had no suitable synonym, 'you may remember a better word for our next meeting and then inform us.'

The critic with the fringe sat down, rather shamed. Father Fóth on the platform shook his head — he was reputed to be a poet and had composed a four part song which was about to be performed. Father Szelényi's hands were still on his stomach, but no longer immobile; he had to hold something in and his fat head was pulled back behind his shoulders because he was shaking with suppressed laughter. He no longer hankered for his cigar but felt highly entertained.

Then followed Erzsi Király's recital. She stepped out in front of the benches in her splendid velvet dress, with the silk inset up to her neck; thick wavy hair brushed to one side. Simple confidence suited her youth, she was aware of all this and played on her own strength. Father Fóth stuck his neck out from behind Sister Gregoria's high veil.

Years earlier, for her exams, Erzsi had recited this favourite poem of Hungarian patriotic literature. She had loved it so much that she learnt it by heart and never forgot it. So there was nothing new to learn, she had only volunteered to recite it because every fourth-year student was expected to perform sometime. She was too lazy for composition in the convent style (for platitudes and a fine conclusion). Actually, of course, she just wanted an excuse to wear *the* dress, to show her friends who were dying to see it.

She did it beautifully, in clear contralto tone, right to the end of the great poem, musical emphasis highlighting the song of the two lute players. The judge acknowledged: 'Learning such a poem is a praiseworthy achievement, but it was a pity she spoke rather than chanted the poem although almost singing in some places.'

Sister Magdolna smiled, flashing her large white teeth. 'You did that very well; that's the right way, in excellent taste.' She spoke simply, nodded and looked at the pupil with encouragement for a few moments.

Many other recitals followed, as well as solos and choir singing. Everyone was hungry by noon when it ended. But the Chaplain waited for Erzsi in the corridor.

'Just a moment young lady!' He did not want to be conspicuous. 'First let me congratulate you. I never knew you had such a fine . . . fine voice for recital. I myself would also have preferred a little more emotion, strength and effect, but your voice is most suitable. I could help you develop your talent for performances.'

'Is that so, Father?' the girl was slightly mocking, but the Chaplain never noticed.

'Most certainly! You can trust me, I know about these things, it's part of my profession. I have a proposal for you which I'll outline now. In a few weeks time our Catholic Boys Club will open. We are going to have a little celebration, only among ourselves, priests and Catholic teachers. I have been asked to write a festive ode — this is what happens if one is reputed to be a poet. I am proposing that you might recite it as your voice is so suitable; of course, I would have to give you some instruction.'

'Oh, Professor, that's hardly possible. An evening occasion, how could I leave the convent? And with whom? I have no acquaintances in the town.'

'That won't matter. My mother will gladly chaperon you and bring you back after the supper. Or, even better, you could spend the night with her, as it will take place on a Saturday. I don't live with my mother.'

'I'm not worried!' interrupted the girl with private amusement. 'But the exeat would have to be given by Kunigunda.'

'Oh, I am not going to argue with her, because . . . because! One will have to ask someone else. I think Virginia, she approves of this sort of thing, it is in accordance with her principles isn't it? "Strengthening the Catholic community." She is the Principal of the teacher training programme, in theory anyway, even though everything is done according to Magdolna's wishes. She won't worry, believe me.'

'If you can make the arrangements, Professor, I should love to help.'

She made her farewell, after 'professoring' him a few more times. As a mere chaplain this title was not due, and meant all the more to him.

So it happened, in spite of Sister Kunigunda's daily blustering, snorting and marshalling. Soon Erzsi started to learn by heart that special ode, which incidentally she despised. It consisted of twenty-eight verses and started like this:

Fight! Act! Row! Stand up to the storm!

Your barque can defeat the waves.
Your Will Power dissolves the fog,
Sun shines forth from behind dark clouds.

And so on and so on. The fourth year crowded round her with curiosity and envy.

'Will there be dancing?' asked Szidu sitting opposite Erzsi in the day room. Immediately she ducked her head down into her history of education book, because the Old One was strolling noisily round the tables with her large rosary.

'All the teachers will be there,' Cornelia gave her opinion, opening wide her lazy dark eyes. 'You'll sit at the same table, and they won't treat you like a schoolgirl but like a young lady at some social gathering. I wonder what they'll talk about? You will tell us everything, won't you?'

'Some people have already outgrown school,' Marika said sarcastically. Ever since she quarrelled with her Chaplain, she had also grown unfriendly towards Erzsi. She called Cornelia a fool behind her back and mixed more with the third-year set.

A week before the performance a large red spot appeared on Erzsi's nose, perhaps from the stuffy atmosphere or from eating too much pastry. Sister Kunigunda gained some childish, mocking satisfaction in watching a pimple grow; but kind Gerolda asked for a little home-made ointment from the pharmacy nuns. The whole dormitory was watching and nursing that spot and rejoiced when by the end of the week it was obviously getting better.

'Erzsi dear, I only want to ask one thing of you.' Cornelia had crept up to her when the place was quiet. 'You can see I don't really care anymore. If, in spite of being such a clever man, he can be so taken in by a girl like Marika, can really believe she is a serious student, genuinely interested in her studies . . . it's not worth bothering with such a man and I am not bothered by him. It's just because I know he is an idealist, a decent person worthy of respect; and perhaps he has had some great sorrow, it's written on his face . . . and purely from friendship. . . .'

'Come on, out with it. What do you want me to do or say? You big baby! Even Janka knew better how to deal with her Paul.'

'I know I am stupid, but there is no need to. . . .'

'Good Lord! You aren't crying, you little fool? Tell me what you want. Shall I bring you a souvenir from Kapossy? A piece of his hair (if only he was not so close shaven!). Or some autograph? A hazelnut that has fallen from his lips during dessert?'

'Oh nothing! Leave me in peace. I don't want everyone to laugh at me.' She went back to her own bed and cried a lot. She was torturing her eyes, rubbing them so hard. Her beauty was so special that Marika looked ordinary by comparison.

Only Helen Gross never approached Erzsi during these weeks. The German girl did not sit on her bed to be interrogated, but seemed serious and reserved, engrossed in her tragic fate and absorbed by her own sorrow.

On Saturday evening Cornelia wanted to help Erzsi change in the cloakroom but the Old One followed her furiously and chased her back to the day room.

'You rubbish! Hurry up. If you are not ready in ten minutes you are not going out anywhere. Shameless hussy!'

Luckily, Erzsi had already done her hair earlier using a hand mirror. She had ordered a bit of powder from the chemist with the help of a day girl; and later when sitting in the coach beside old Mrs Fóth she deftly dabbed her spot, then at an opportune moment, quick as lightning, she undid her white silk breast inlay and shoved it into her pocket. A heart-shaped opening, not too low, made her gown appropriate for the occasion. Erzsi could relax and enjoy her youth.

How nice it would be, she thought to herself conscientiously remembering her friend, if *he* were here tonight to see me. But it will be fun anyhow. I shall get a good supper. If only that stupid poem were not so long. *If the floral beauty of the green island beckons, do not regard the reef!* Damn! I must smile at *floral beauty,* and at *green island* look around festively.

'More festively! It suits you young lady!' the poet had urged her during the rehearsals.

NINE

The hall of the new club was a typical provincial building, with its floor of bare boards, and platform balanced on packing cases. Assembled in the rows of ill-assorted chairs were: girls dressed in white and their starched mammas; 'faithful' Catholic boys slightly sweaty in their Sunday best; lots of priests; and sixth formers from the grammar school, by permission of their Headmaster, with some of their teachers. On the platform, Erzsi, restraining her mischievous mood and composing herself, recited all twenty-eight verses as the poet had desired, to their conclusion (thank heaven): 'Festively, very festively!'

> But we have a magnet: Hope
> Which leads us: The Strong Will!

She ended (as all things have to) relieved no line had been omitted, or rhyming couplet confused; apart from the poet no one would have noticed or cared.

Then followed a Haydn string quartet — Oh!; performed by fifth formers with their teacher — 'would have satisfied the most discerning critic,' said the church paper next day. The star of the local theatre spoke a dramatic monologue. Around her neck she wore a thin gold-plated chain with a little cross; Reverend Fóth, as secretary of the new club, had carefully marked the purple passages of the script for her. Pretty Mrs Holzer, the teacher's wife, played the piano, and a little girl recited a ballad (this was really charming, an eight-year-old puppet primadonna); a thin lady in a gaudy dress played folk songs on the cymbalo. Such trials and vicissitudes led to the happy haven of supper.

After introductions and congratulations Mrs Fóth, still bemused by her son's success, placed Erzsi comfortably between herself and the poet priest.

'Do you like fish?' asked her neighbour on the left who was struggling between two personas: teacher and entertaining host. 'The bones are unpleasant, but every rose has a thorn; charming young ladies are the only exception to that rule.'

'Do you mean among fish, Professor?'

'You enjoy teasing me! Among roses — of course, the souls of girls need to be pure and spotless.'

'And they must smell sweet,' replied Erzsi in boredom and pressed her bouquet to her face. 'Might you, Professor, perhaps be considered as a gardener among the flower souls of young girls?'

'You are referring to my job as teacher of religion and morals at the Institute? It's no easy task to understand the minds of young girls.'

'Even for a poet?'

'That means nothing I assure you, and even makes things harder because poetry nourishes imagination. To discover the thoughts hidden behind the foreheads of the girls. . . .'

'Spoils things?'

'No, I did not say that. Just confuses. They are all trying to hide their feelings. What a lot of moods they have, a lot of moods. Look at yourself!'

'In the first place, I have to tell you, I am no longer such a very young girl, I am twenty-two years old and have outgrown these moods. And secondly, we must talk generally and not take examples from present company.' Erzsi had her own reasons for spinning out this pointless conversation. 'We have plenty of common acquaintances, my class mates, who are all three or four years younger and better suited for testing your theory. I wonder, Professor, which among them you consider moody?'

'You don't have to look far for examples,' said the young priest suspiciously. 'There are many foolish ones among them, a lot of good qualities and charm as well. For example in your class. . . .'

'What about Marika Pável?' Erzsi suggested boldly. 'I know the nuns (who have been bringing her up since early childhood) consider her particularly difficult, wild, passionate, vain and careless. That is the accepted view of her and all the waters of the Danube cannot wash her clean. But do consider, Professor, the psychology of her case. Marika grew up without a mother, her morose old father lives at an isolated ugly station. She never had brothers or sisters or relatives, came young to the convent.'

'Ah yes, I thought as much,' agreed the young man. His suspicions were allayed by the serious tone of Erzsi's conversation. She was obviously ignorant of his little indiscretions with Marika. 'To be honest I have always thought the nuns were not dealing with her in the right way. Not sufficiently individually, taking her personality into account.'

'They have alienated her. That child has deep feelings she will not allow herself to show but hides in childish, foolish ways. I know her. She is a most interesting young person.'

'Is that so? My knowledge of human nature led me to similar conclusions. I like to treat the young souls in my care very individually. Allow me to fill your glass?'

Oh you stupid fool! — Erzsi said to herself and almost out loud. She observed the face of the young man becoming more flushed. Their conversation took a serious turn and Erzsi noticed he had stopped looking into the heart-shaped opening of her dress. Men are quite decent, she thought, even the naughtiest of them have more honesty and faith than seventeen-year-old dressed-in-blue convent girls. She clicked her glass and drank.

'Yes,' she continued with conviction, 'our Marika needs gentle, sensitive handling. That would bring out many worthwhile qualities in her young personality. She has a lovely temperament.'

'She is so innocent.'

'And yet quite serious. I value her discretion most. She is an incredibly reliable person. She won't ever gossip about things that might implicate someone else. That's important among girls, especially in a convent.'

'Undoubtedly, undoubtedly! Quite essential for beneficial teaching. Will you have another drink with me, young lady? Thank you for your helpful information. I shall consider it my duty to make use of it as a teacher. Because, because. . . .'

They were shushing for silence at the head of the table, the waiters had stopped changing the plates. Toasts followed, speeches, broken phrases: *the Association — cooperation — intimate circle — indefatigable — the kind nest — joys of friendship — our much respected Chairman — I give you the toast.* Clinking of glasses, drinking and the next speaker cleared his throat: *most grateful — true cultural event — moral standards — religious spirit — worthwhile endeavour;* glasses clicked again, loud *hear hear*s and the clatter of plates, talk and laughter.

Erzsi noticed her neighbour looking dazed and sentimental, in the early stage of intoxication. He had drunk this strong unfamiliar wine too quickly. He'll have had enough, she thought. She had observed the guests to be a slightly rougher crowd than she was accustomed to in her home town; a matter of chance. The backdrop of small traders with smoking room standards seemed below the outward elegance of priestly manners. No matter, she thought, all the more fun. She asked permission from her hostess to change places and sit by Mrs Holzer, whom she had got to know during the evening.

This pretty German wife appeared to be well bred and pleasant. She and her husband sat at a table with a group of bachelor teachers. She was delighted to see Erzsi and monopolized her for a while. When the pudding arrived they reached the point Erzsi had been waiting for, their joint acquaintance, Helen Gross.

'You know, my dear, I am a very good Catholic, as converts usually are (particularly when one starts with love of one's husband and then finds conviction, as I have done), and I like religious vocation; had I not met Józsi, it would have suited my temperament to become a nun. The late Reverend Mother was my ideal of a woman, my godmother, such a wise person. . . . But, you know, what they are doing now with young Helen is not to my taste, it's unpleasant. Józsi and I have talked about it. We are sure the nuns would not cherish the girl in this way if she were poor. It's useless anyway, I know she has no desire, not a scrap of what they call *vocation* to become a nun. Can it be forced upon her? That would surely be a sin, Józsi agrees with me. Reverend Mother told her "only if it is your sincere vocation". I can hardly wait for the end of this mourning — the old terrors won't even let me speak with her! Her wonderful old aunt (whom I visited on her death bed) asked me to keep an eye on Helen.'

Erzsi wanted to hurry on to the heart of the matter, remarking:

'Don't you think it likely, even though it might be against her true feelings, that Helen will remain in the convent?'

'Aren't they just forcing her? She will never be happy there, she has told me so quite sincerely. She is a grown up young woman of twenty and has lived out in the world. She mustn't let herself be bullied by those old women.'

'You can't just blame old nuns when a young woman lets her fancy roam.'

'What are you saying? What are you trying to imply? Has she a lover, some young man? She has not confided in me though I am usually sympathetic about these things. Was it some one back in Bavaria?'

'No, absolutely not.'

'Are you serious! Is she caught up by some teacher, one of the priests?'

'Oh absolutely not!'

'Please don't tease me. She never travelled anywhere except to visit us once a month. I must learn about her feelings. I know a very decent suitable fellow for her. Recently I ascertained his serious intentions for our young Helen. . . . Well, I have to know about her side too, our quiet introvert Bavarian girl who never went anywhere else — apart from him she could not have met any other man, unless it is my husband.'

'She is not in love with your husband; I can take an oath on that!'

'Ah, then all is well. My dear, you can tell her tomorrow, so she need not spoil her eyes with tears, some girls enjoy crying, I did. All is well. Toffler is serious and reliable like most Germans. His background is alright too; I know because he is Józsi's best friend. He has a slightly jealous temperament and strict standards in love and marriage. Years ago he broke off an engagement for that reason. He has just won a permanent teaching job, not too high a salary, Helen would be a good match. Toffler has no inkling about her fortune.'

'Do tell him soon. Such ideas are no *impediment* to marriage.'

'Not at all. He is a bit naïve in these matters. All will be well. We have to help them a bit, these young lovers are so stupid, aren't they? You and I have some common sense. She is a pretty girl, don't you think, with her large brown eyes? Her skin is not as clear as yours but that sort of thing often improves with marriage. Oh, I am happy. If Toffler only knew what we are talking about.'

'Is he here? Which is he?'

'Over there, diagonally across from the director and my husband. A good profile don't you think?'

Erzsi was satisfied with the appearance of the fair-haired, blue-eyed, bearded young man. 'Like a romantic hero,' she reflected kindly, then sat quietly for a few moments, looking at the company now eating their tarts.

'Tell me,' she asked Mrs Holzer, 'do you know our teacher of educational methods, Kapossy? Is he a friend of yours? Could you entice him over here?'

'He is a fascinating priest, with his dark face.' Mrs Holzer laughed and asked father Kapossy to join their table for dessert.

The priest did not feel comfortable next to Erzsi,

except when she was talking to her other neighbour. He did not know what to ask or say to this composed adult pupil. Her mocking smile disturbed him — in class he tended politely to ignore her. Embarrassed, he looked at her evening bag.

'Is this hand work?'

'It's Slovak work from our district,' she explained and shook it so clumsily, all the contents fell out.

'Quite a collection,' Kapossy murmured with his aesthetic dry smile. 'What a lot of things. Needles, thread, notebook, pencil, ribbons. What about that folded paper, what does that hide?'

'Oh dear, that is secret,' she flustered and reached after it, more like a teenager than a mature twenty-two-year-old.

'What? Not allowed to your teacher, to me?'

His strange dark smile awkwardly mocked the young woman as he slapped his hand over the crumpled paper. He had drunk some wine at supper, but not to excess.

'Oh no please don't, you shouldn't!' pleaded Erzsi. 'How could I have left that there? Please return it to me, Professor.'

'What if I do not?' He spoke more harshly, his hard eyes starting to flame. 'You must have some reason to be so alarmed. You tremble. I have the right to know, as your teacher. . . . Is it something personal, to do with me?'

'Oh no — that is to say. . . . It's difficult for me to lie to you, Professor, but I cannot give you that piece of paper. Probably something childish, I didn't write it, it's in my bag by chance. I don't want to compromise a friend, or make trouble for someone else. Precisely because you are our teacher. I'd rather be blamed now.'

'So it's honour among friends, is that it? Girls have

that too I know. Well let's start by way of diplomacy. If I promise that no one will get into trouble for this, and I read it not as your teacher but out of idle curiosity. What then?'

'Oh my God! The thing is I don't know what is written there myself. It was during a lesson — you know, Professor, even the older girls play pranks and throw notes to each other when they get bored. Marika Pável threw this to Szidu, I caught it and rather meanly kept it, and forgot about it.'

'Oh,' said the teacher blushing slightly at the mention of Marika's name. 'Then you can give it to me quite legitimately if you do not know the text. I promise you I will read it unofficially at home — with my interest in psychology — is that all right? It will be of no consequence to anyone. Does that satisfy you, young lady?'

He had already pocketed the blue squared maths note paper, with a strange grabbing movement. Erzsi fell silent. She looked anxious and downcast though she was merely tired and ready to leave, utterly bored. . . . I didn't have much fun; but then that's the way it should be, as I am no longer free to flirt. I suppose there was some entertainment, they gave us a good supper and I saw lots of painfully awful dresses.

She, of course, knew exactly what was written on that silly note:

> Szidu!
> What do you say to our rotten Erzsi. She is going out tonight for a soirée and, with her mature charms, will conquer our dear priests. The Devil take her! She'd better leave my Fóth alone. Not that I'm jealous — she only flirts with him since we quarrelled, I can't complain. Next lesson I

mean to make up with him. He is the handsomest of them all. I only flirted with that creep Kapossy out of pique, anyway he bores me. I can't keep up the serious moral student forever. I've had enough. I'll leave him to that fool Popescu, who suits him, let her gaze into the moonlight and cry secretly for him. He is such an old idiot he does not recognize or make use of her beauty.
Write back to me, Bye.

Erzsi could hardly believe her own powers as an actress, how easy it all was in one evening 'to wrap up the whole world'.

She was relieved when Mrs Fóth suggested they leave — the priests could not drink after midnight because of mass the following morning. She returned early next morning to the convent and avoided Kunigunda's anger. On her way she managed to pass the main post office and send some letters *poste restante* to Budapest. One was addressed to Paul Eördögh, Lawyer, Debrecen.

While she was changing Gidu ran up to her.

'Lots of news since yesterday. Helen puts on her postulant collar today; she went last night to Berchtolda, crying all the time, but Berchtolda was not cross with her. And yesterday I saw Emerika without a black apron. The mourning ended on 20th February, and the Bishop has announced that the day for the election will be at the beginning of April. It will take time to prepare for all the visitors from the sister houses who'll be coming to vote and have to stay here. I must dash, the Old One is yelling!'

'That idiot Helen! That fool of a Helen! That bungler Helen!' repeated Erzsi as she put on her blue uniform again.

TEN

'What's up then mate? Hey look, they've hauled down their bloody flag at their convent.'

'No! I wish the whole damned place would crash down about their heads.'

Two drunk farmers sat in one of the rooms of The Pipers Inn. They wore small waistcoats, riding breeches, leather leggings; they had short grey hair, tanned bony faces, coarse moustaches, work hardened hands. Probably from a village some distance away, they were here for the famous cattle auctions: arguing and bargaining all day with other traders; having a great time. A great time: plenty of good wine, banknotes and gypsy music; that's how it should be, without women, just the two of them in good Hungarian style. Now, in the early hours, the gypsy band had stopped playing and started drinking cheap homebrewed wine, their largesse from these two gentlemen; pouring the sour drink down their parched throats and gobbling paprika stew. Peace descended: wine fumes mingled with sweat, manure and onion in a heavy fug. The two drunk faces came closer together. At times they found speaking difficult, their rare utterances ever more earthy and obscene. At first they had felt full of themselves, showing off, arrogant as peacocks; then more depressed, downcast. These two posing as 'gentlemen' reverted to their usual ways.

'Why worry about those old maids? Let'em manage their own problems!'

'Problems?' His stupefied, drunken anger started again. 'Why do they lock themselves up then? Let 'em come here, I'd soon fix their problems!' He swore. The gypsies at the far table were enjoying his performance.

'Fool! I know what you really mean. It's more than ten years ago — your wife's dead — but you haven't forgotten or forgiven that other thing. One drink and you remember Sara Komoróczy, the Lord Lieutenant's daughter. Come, confess! You're thinking of her. You can't do a bloody thing about it. She's sleeping a hundred paces from you, or saying her prayers — you can see their church from here, look. She's called herself Adele as a Bride of Christ. She sleeps with Christ out of spite for Laci Békássy. Remember him? He thought she was his, the same class, educated, a good lawyer; she called you 'dung mover' because you were crazy about horses, and dropped out of class. Everyone in our village talked about it. We all know you asked to marry her *again* when Laci jilted her. You couldn't win her even then. She chose Jesus, not you, out of spite!'

He was really drunk and stupid. The other became incensed by the smut of his insinuations, and bitterness broke out without restraint.

'I swear to God I'm going there right now, and we'll see!'

'Where the hell will you go at this time?'

'Where? Into the nuns, to three-hundred-and-fifty virgins! I'll find Sara. She'll speak different now!'

'Fool! We are both drunk as pigs. Let's go home. Or somewhere better to drink.'

'Don't "fool" me. I'm going there, inside the place, right now, as I am! You'll see. I swear to you, straight up. You can laugh. Let's bet. You daren't take me on? Now. For real money, one hundred koronas. You daren't? You're well known for being too mean. Your wife makes you kneel on potatoes if you don't give her money!'

'Are you talking about me? You can take that back, for a start. . . . So anyway. What's that you said? Inside — just knocking at the gate and running away won't count. They have to see you spend a bit of time in there. Who'll witness it? Shall I come?'

'You wait right here. You'd be a nuisance. Let the band come, all three of them. I'm going there, staying in there for a while. I'll see what Sara does now, what she looks like. If I get into the convent, stay five minutes, the money's mine. Come on you. Shut up the lot of you or I'll bash your brains out!'

'You're going to bribe that lot to tell your story!'

'Word of honour as a gentleman. You'll read it in the paper tomorrow. Then you'll be satisfied. Come on then. I'll need a coach instead of my cart. A covered coach to ride against the cold March wind.'

He seemed to have sobered up, become purposeful after all the stupidity. The wager itself fired him up, not the money. He could gamble twice as much in an evening. His reputation, not his former love, spurred him on.

ELEVEN

The hired coach drew up quietly by the wall a few yards from the convent gate. The three gypsy youths held their breath and ducked low. A figure in a dark travelling coat pulled at the bell and waited, pressed close to the building.

'Who is that?' A young woman's voice from within enquired.

'The postman. Express delivery. I'm bringing a telegram for the convent.'

The sentry nun put her key into the lock. Hearing the humble voice of an old man, she had no suspicion of evil. She was a young novice, sleepy, inexperienced, and quite dazed by incessant prayer. During this interregnum registered letters and telegrams were frequent; there was more coming and going than usual. The key turned in the lock, the nun stepped aside to reach for the message. Next moment, terrified, deathly pale, she shrieked out the names of all the saints.

His cloak fell off and dropped outside onto the

threshold. A hateful phantom streaked past the young nun along the corridor and back towards the stairs; with the same wild motion, it sped towards the ground floor kitchens. Petrified like Lot's wife, sufficiently recovered to think only of herself, she fled with childish despair. Like a squirrel she leapt up the wide stairs, oblivious of her long clothes and their inherent dignity. Without pausing at the first floor, she rushed up to where the nuns slept in cubicles surrounded by white curtains down to the floor. She pushed open the first door with a heart rending shriek:

'Robbers! Murder! A Man. . . a madman in the convent!'

Leaving the door open she ran to the next room. All this was happening in the right wing of the convent where the teaching and working nuns lived. Within minutes the corridor was filled with frightened figures wringing their hands; wisps of hair peeked out from under the hastily donned veils; in this incomprehensible situation even the wisest nuns lost their composure. Whispering and uncertain they gathered at the top of the stairs.

'Where? Perhaps she's imagined it, for Heaven's sake!' Some started to cry, none dared to descend. There was no hint of a sound from the first floor.

The two wings were separated by the chapel, with only the choir gallery opening onto the second-floor corridor. Here two steps led up to a small alcove framing a Gothic window and the statue of a mild paternal St Joseph. The night watchwoman, lamp in hand, was striding past (deep obeisance towards the chapel). She came from the left wing, where the old nuns slept. She had performed the usual duties of checking the dying embers of the stoves, had looked-in on the elderly sleeping nuns in case one fell ill and needed help. She now approached the corridor with firm steps, her habit in perfect order, and viewed with astonishment the hullabaloo; walking faster, she raised her lamp. It was Adele, formerly Sara Komoróczy.

'What has happened? What? Where? Who? When? . . . Good Lord, and all you do is stand here? Anyone could go up the other stairs or through the chapel to our sleeping pupils above. We must divide into three groups — you stay here, and you go by the back stairs. The rest follow me. We have to see if there really is anyone. Light every lamp, have lights everywhere.'

They began their descent, more bravely, together in their groups. All realized they must defend the honour of their convent, their young and old, their peace and perhaps their lives. From all sides these enthusiastic fighters advanced, hurrying, puffing. Sara Komoróczy, southern aristocrat who was not so easily frightened, led the way.

'Let's have a look at this robber, this madman! Was there only one? I wonder if he's hiding somewhere? Let's get him out. Do you think he'll try to cause trouble again? Come on, let's see.'

Then they all stopped for just one second, as the ugly and appalling silhouette of the intruder flickered into view, candle lit in front of a dark image. Adele focused on the shiny object in his right hand: might it be a revolver? No — if she could trust her eyes it was a pocket watch. He was standing still counting the minutes.

'Now we will catch him!' shouted Adele in triumph. 'He won't escape this time! Lock the gate. Oh! Oh, it's wide open. Shut it, then he can't get out. Jancsi, Miska, Tráján. Get up! Do your duty.'

Panting she rushed out into the wet March night, to the courtyard, by the well and into the next yard, by the hospice. Labourers lived between the stables and the gardener's cottage. It must have been ten years since Adele had been given such a chance to rush about.

'Get up you lazy dogs! Cowards! Quick, bring ropes. . . .'

But by the time the sleepers arrived with rope the horrid apparition was far away. He, of course, never got beyond the ground floor, rushing foolishly among the dark images. Then he stopped, looked around, disconcerted by the unfamiliar surroundings, his own large ugly shadow revealed by the night light, the silence, narrow corridors; on the walls another male figure, naked, pale, in deathly immobility — bleeding, mild, blessedly familiar, there — on the crucifix. He was startled, his teeth began to chatter, he felt cold; stubborn and groggy, he waited by the lamp; blind and deaf to anything else, he started to count the seconds.

Suddenly he heard the row, steps approaching, a woman's voice (once familiar to him); but still twenty seconds were needed, now fifteen, yes. At last. Time's up? Get out now! Quicker than lightning, by the same route he came. The porta was open, no one ran to shut it or trap him. No one came after him, the three groups became silent again in the dark corridors. Their leader was urging battle out in the courtyard: all in vain — they did not want this prisoner of war, they would rather he escaped. Outside the gypsy band leader offered him his fur cloak.

Jancsi, Miska and Tráján still stood there with a long rope, but the intruder had already received the reward of his wager.

The ant heap continued its nervous agitation long after this jolt from the outside world. The corridors were crowded, everyone had seen it; those who had slept through such a memorable five minutes were in retrospect outraged, discussing the matter even more fearfully. The most likely theory was a madman; difficult to imagine any other possibility. Further away, on the Lourdes corridor they talked of several intruders, some had seen three. A novice reminded them of the terrifying tales about Jack the Ripper. Last of all the left wing stirred as these stories spread; pale, with stiff faces, the old German nuns stood around; accusing eyes turned on the younger nuns with whom they lived uneasily; nodding in mutual sympathy, they could not explain what had happened.

'Ach Jessus! Um Gottes Willen! Jessus-Maria-Joseph!' could be heard on all sides.

Geralda, in charge of the young students, remembered to hasten upstairs to the third floor where they all slept in both wings, which on this floor were separate and opposite each other. There was still complete silence, but the sound of her footsteps startled a couple who were whispering. In night-dresses, skirts, shawls and slippers, like paupers they had a rendezvous out on the cold corridor. They were not, as might have been suspected, secret lovers. No, it was Erzsi Király and Helen Gross the new postulant, daring all the dangers, discussing highly important matters in the silence of the night.

'What is this Erzsi? Why are you here? Out in the corridor at this time? Who was that postulant? Or do you all know the news by now?'

'Yes dear Mother!' Erzsi lied easily, without any idea of what she knew.

'Appalling isn't it! Such depravity! A man at such an hour. What will become of us, if this sort of thing can happen?'

'A thief!' guessed Erzsi intuitively, surprised. 'Terrible!' she continued. 'A postulant rushed over just now, I don't even know her name, I happened to be out here, but none of the others know anything yet.'

'Don't disturb them Erzsi, let them sleep in peace.'

Naturally Erzsi told everyone she possibly could. On that cold night by the statue she had actually planned to pass on certain messages of love, making young Helen unbelievably happy:

'Yes, he really does love you. Get that into your silly head. He loves you not me. Yes just as you do him. Is that so incredible? Maybe it is strange and perhaps not so strange, but here is the letter from Mrs Holzer for you; the fourth-year girl from town brought it in, you know that dull girl who lives with Mrs Fóth. But for Heaven's sake be careful, hide it! So your lover has declared himself! He wants to get you out, O-U-T! He wants to marry you, M-A-R-R-Y Y-O-U! And lots more. You little bride of the convent, the question now is how?'

'How to do it? Oh my God!'

'We'll have to sort it all out. You in here in the dormitory for postulants, Toffler out there in cold bachelor digs, dreaming of you, when sooner or later you must sleep together!'

'Oh Erzsi, you're so hard headed. I really can't think of anything now. I am so happy. Everything is all right, I am so happy. I can't comprehend a thing.'

'What's the difficulty? Go and visit Mrs Holzer as soon as you can. She'll invite you most kindly to stay during the period of your engagement. You'll have to get your trousseau together. Don't you dare show yourself to your betrothed in these horrible postulant clothes! Tell Mother Berchtolda tomorrow, as soon as possible.'

'Oh Erzsi, I haven't got the courage to do that.'

'Are you mad? You haven't got the courage? Don't

you want to become Mrs Toffler? Don't you want your skin spots to clear up? Do you really want to become a nun?'

'Oh no! I never really wanted to . . . but now I am here and I've started the process.'

'*Get out* I tell you. Even fully fledged priests and nuns have got out.'

'Yes, but . . . I can't tell them. What will Mother Berchtolda say? She has been so very kind. I've told her about my sad love and broken heart. And Simonea and Leona, the old nuns, what would they say? My aunt has appeared in their dreams — no I cannot do it.'

'How absurd! How will you manage to get out then? Does that have to be my task too? They'll expel me from the teacher's course, my poor mother will be in despair.'

'Oh don't be cross with me, Erzsi! You always know what to do.'

'You want to be smuggled out, that's more romantic, and then you don't have to do a thing. . . . Go back to sleep and dream now. We'll think about it tomorrow, but we must act soon. Damn, they are coming, it's only Geralda. Run!'

Then the next day Father Szelényi stopped young Helen in the corridor by the porta, smiling his fat cigar smile, asking her with masculine malice:

'Well Helen, what happened during the night?'

The postulant turned pale, began trembling and then burst into tears. The old priest's all seeing love of gossip was legendary. The German girl believed he was hinting at her pre-dawn secret conversation (for it was in her mind all the time) . . . that somehow he already knew she was loved; she was loved . . . and was planning disloyally to leave the convent for the sake of a man.

TWELVE

What happened that night? The title of a well-known operetta headlined the story in the local 'liberal' newspaper. The same paper had often reported unkindly on the internal affairs of the convent. They took the opportunity again; while pretending to treat the story with care, there was much hypocrisy evident: shock at 'the mindless intrusion' and 'Casanova decadence'. Reading between the lines, it was written tongue-in-cheek; finding the prank 'novel', witty, the editorial staff seemed to envy the perpetrator of the incident. The shock and the impact were painted at length and in detail; night visitors to the convent were the talk of the town for a week. No one could discover who had made this wager. The men must have fled far by morning; and the three gypsies kept silent, not liking questions from the law; the nuns did not lodge a complaint. In fact, the Bishop's newsletter resolutely played down the affair ('a drunk and disorderly individual had pulled the bell by mistake' was its entire report). The civic authorities, not sure about the suspects' identities were in no hurry to investigate the case. Who knew what trouble that might cause? — like stirring up a wasps' nest.

Within the walls the real storm broke, and the dust flew for some time after the night's visitation. Everyone was shocked, talking about it in the parlour, in the retirement wing, in the novitiate dormitory; they whispered and giggled on the benches of the school room in front of the gossiping day girls. After a few days Mother Simonea, formerly Mistress of the Novitiates, sister of the previous Reverend Mother, called the whole community together in the parlour of the retirement wing. Everyone knew she was the one who was campaigning, writing letters, agitating, busybodying secretly in favour of electing the strict Leona, sister of the Founder Reverend Mother. She had been doing this for a long time with as much intensity as the younger Hungarian nuns canvassed for their candidate. Nevertheless, neither Virginia nor Berchtolda dared miss the meeting. You never could tell what might happen behind your back, if you weren't present. Better to be face to face.

'We old ones have been watching silently and patiently for a long time', started Simonea, 'the liberties which began during the last days of our lately departed Mother. We cannot stand by silently any longer without protest, for the results of these new ideas are now evident. What will become of us, dear Sisters? What will be the reputation of our Order and of our convent? Will we be receiving night visitors henceforth? Will agnostic reporters and wicked Jews sharpen their pens at our expense? I do not propose to investigate who might be the "well-born and well-heeled aristocratic Hungarian girl" who unwittingly seems to have been the excuse for this shameful occurrence. I do know that none of my contemporaries who came to join this convent from afar had any worldly past. I don't want to talk about that. I merely want to ask that all of you, in the interest of our Order, heed me with the respect due to my age. I would ask, until the election, when we will find a new leader with God's help, that all of us, by firm example and adherence to our rules, try to prevent any repetition of so shameful an event, which has irreparably harmed our good reputation. I would like to remind you of the wisdom which Sister Leona used to instill in us; perhaps we should have paid greater heed to her words, namely: true convent life can only be lived with total rigour, following the example of the saints. If we ourselves deviate even slightly from the hard path, we open a door to frivolity and unrestrained evil. Recent events show us how right she is; anyone who enters here must devote her whole life and soul to Jesus. *You cannot mix these things*; those who are not suitable for our life should stay out in the world. It is perfectly possible to lead a God-fearing life there; we here may then be fewer, but true followers of Our Lord. "Many are chosen but few are called", as it is written in the Scriptures.'

A moment of silence followed her words; Virginia and Berchtolda silently bowed their heads; they began to realize how clever this old woman was (much more so than her nominated candidate Leona), how skilfully she was exploiting this unfortunate event to serve her own purpose.

'Yes, yes! You are right, so right, dear Sister!' Kunigunda agreed loudly and nodded her head. Her face flushed as red as a cardinal's hat. Glancing at her, Virginia's sarcastic mouth showed contempt.

Virginia then spoke carefully, diplomatically. No one was really to blame for these recent scandalous events. Moreover she pointed out — she wanted to avoid giving offence — that they were all equally keen to prevent further mishaps. She would suggest that in future only older and more experienced nuns should take on night duty. There was further discussion from both sides. Prudent Berchtolda checked her followers from strong outbursts; she realized it would be foolish to poison the mood at such a time. Finally they agreed some procedure for the election; to withdraw from postulants their monthly exeat, to stop their contacts with day girls, and also stop contacts between candidates and boarders. All this was as a result of foolish gossip following the ugly incident. Furthermore, the *silencium* must be adhered to more strictly. Care must be taken that the student teachers do not hang about after their lessons or remain in the classrooms. (This only referred to the very young ones. Simonea smiled to Virginia, whose mouth twitched in its usual tell-tale way). Nobody could have explained how these salutary regulations would in future prevent two drunkards at The Pipers Inn planning wild pranks and making crazy bets. It was best to remain silent and not mention such heresies.

'What a miserable state of affairs,' Virginia puckered her forehead, walking away with Berchtolda. 'Will there be even more unpleasant consequences from this ghastly affair? Do you think, dear Sister, they have sent out wildly exaggerated descriptions in their letters to the sister houses?'

'Never mind, but let's be on our guard,' answered Berchtolda, also agitated. 'After all they mean well, dear Sister. We must have faith that God is with us.'

'True, but they believe God is with them.'

The next day Szidu and Gidu cried their eyes out in the parlour. They were supposed to take some drawing materials from the post room, where the supplier had deposited them, up to Emerika; but Kunigunda just would not allow it, scolding them mercilessly. In the new building they could continue to chat with day girls because the teaching nuns were still lax about the new regime; in the old building, particularly with the postulants, it was quite impossible to exchange a single word. Erzsi Király tried, with great danger to herself, to have a few minutes conversation with Helen. The Old One kept her owl-like vigil throughout the night, frequently patrolling the dormitories. Geralda felt too frightened to turn a blind eye. During these weeks the perceived distance between different parts of the convent became greater, as did the separation of groups by their different uniforms. Passions that had begun to die down during the liberal period were now fanned back into flame. The mere sight, far along the corridor, of a novice veil or postulant collar would again cause feverish shivers in a young boarder; as formerly, before the infection of this modern, prosaic notion of 'simple friendship' (no one knowing whence it originated) had spread through the convent.

'My dear friend, I cannot write as often as before,' wrote Erzsi from a more secret spot than the stove, 'they guard us like bandits. It's only three or four months until I win my silly diploma. I have to get down to serious study from geology through to methodology and all the other "ologies". I would like to help the Bavarian girl, Helen, to get married too. Honestly, these are the kind of things that preoccupy me in this convent; though I would much prefer to fly for a morning to the banks of the Danube, better still into the House to hear you give an important speech. That's on Tuesday; until then it's finance, isn't it? (I keep well informed. The girl who brings in your letters deserves a box of truffles at Easter, she brings in the paper every day. Sometimes she can only cut out the council report column. If you only knew how difficult it is for me to read it, but I always manage.) You know you must arrange for me to be posted to Budapest, eventually. In the provinces they will never leave us in peace! Please come to fetch me after the exam. It will be wonderful to fly into your arms free as a bird immediately after the *Te Deum.* I still have to think about whether I can then come to Budapest for a couple of days. You know one has to get used to wild thoughts of freedom. As I've said before: when I am truly independent, earning my living, my own boss, I can be properly responsible for myself, my deeds and my own decisions.

'Sadly, I'm not going to be in that position with this absurd little diploma paper. The lovely dress pattern you sent me (that was really sweet of you) will still have to be paid for by my mother. (I will not consider any other way, that's final.) They'll give me a good job, and I will work hard, I promise you; as well as anyone else, if not better. One takes on responsibilities with a paid job, and I enjoy teaching and children and observing life. I haven't been so earnest with you before, have I? Anyway, no rush, there's no need to hurry as the old porter told us when we ran for the train last winter, thinking we'd miss it: We Have Time! The same is true for you, dear friend. Forty years, so what? I'm already in my twenty-third year, as you'll see! Goodbye, it's getting cold here, only the last flicker of the wick, and the smell from the postulants' shoes stored in this cupboard. If I were caught . . . believe me I am playing with danger here just as much as at home: when I told my mother I had a toothache (if you remember?); and even had a good tooth removed so that I could get out and have the chance to keep my appointment with you. She had become so suspicious poor soul, but I didn't want you to wait in vain. I'm still a bit crazy about life and you; I fear the ink is freezing to the nib. God Bless my Darling, God Bless you.'

Strangely, only the contact between females of different groups, and their possible *forbidden affections,* was so strictly prohibited and guarded against; and this served only to fascinate and titillate the sharp eye. No one seemed to care that Marika was often over in Father Fóth's classroom before theology lessons, explaining that she had not done her homework because of a headache; and then the two of them would come in flushed and late. The class had got used to this renewal of their old games. Out in the world it would be called flirtation. Only Erzsi observed Kapossy, after a lesson in methodology, turning quietly and muttering between his lips:

'Would you be so kind as to bring these essays to me in my study, Miss Popescu?'

For brown-eyed Cornelia the world turned upside-down. For a moment her tired eyes looked at him; then her whole proud bearing recovered, suddenly a fiery look blazed beneath her beautiful long lashes; she straightened up like a reed, her steps became springy, light like a gazelle . . . Erzsi watched them both and smiled.

THIRTEEN

Troubles seldom come singly; they recognize a hospitable home and keep the door open. Barely two weeks had elapsed before the next misfortune befell the convent, hard to explain and most untoward — just as old Simonea had warned.

It arrived in the guise of two mendicant sisters who wore brown-striped linen cloaks, rough black hairy hoods and long muddy boots; tough customers from the poorest strata of society. They had come on foot through the spring mud, with their large awkward haversacks, and, as was customary, took lodgings in the convent's smaller guest room. All day they roamed the town collecting for poor orphan children; but they were punctual for meals. Pupils coming towards the pair going along the ill-lit corridors would laugh (in spite of Kunigunda's grumbling from behind). These two were strange, one of them especially, so squat and with such a broad face. Many of the young girls ran to kiss their hands, because there is merit in showing humility to the most lowly of God's brides.

One of the postulants was assigned to sleep with the guests in their room. It was her duty to make up the beds and clean the room for them. As she was due for watch duties on the third night, Berchtolda found another girl to take her place — who happened to come from a distant village on the frontier. This young girl came to Berchtolda the next morning, obviously most disturbed.

'Dear Mother, I wish to tell you something!'

'Later my dear, when we go up. We must have quiet near the chapel until mass is finished and must not break the morning *silencium* without cause.'

'Yes but — but, I have an important matter to tell you.'

'What is it dear child? You are trembling? What is the matter? Tell me!

'Those mendicant nuns in the guest rooms . . . they are not nuns.'

'What do you mean? What are they? Oh dear! You slept there last night? What do you know? Tell me!'

'Dear Mother, they are not even women, only one of them is.'

'Nonsense! What are you talking about? Are you dreaming? That can't be. . . . What on earth. . . ? Now calmly and sensibly.'

'I can understand Ruthenian, because it's the language of the poor in my home district. I heard them talking and counting their money in the night . . . they are . . . imposters, a married couple.'

'Impossible!'

'I'm absolutely sure. I heard everything; they didn't realize I could understand their language, as I'd just replaced the Hungarian girl of the previous nights. I pretended to be asleep behind my curtain. They are a couple of Galician railway workers who collect the money for their own pockets. They are packing up now to move on; but we could still catch them.'

'Now? Oh no! How do you know they are . . . a couple?'

The little postulant hung her head in silence.

'Oh you poor, poor dear, my sweet child!' Berchtolda's maternal worried concern overwhelmed her. She gently caressed the head of the young girl, who broke down in tears hiding her face in her handkerchief.

'My dear girl, for the love of Heaven why did you not come to me at once, wake me or one of the other nuns?'

'I was frightened, and taken by surprise, these sort of people may have knives, and oh . . . I was so ashamed!'

'Now tell me the truth,' the nun's questioning voice was trembling, 'did anyone harm you, your body, or touch you?'

'Oh no, not me!' protested the girl vigorously.

'Be thankful; your guardian angels and saints protected you. Oh dear! We'll probably have another scandal, a shock like last time. What a time of trial we are having! The most important thing now is to keep this to ourselves. Let the guilty run away; we will trust God to punish them. Don't tell anyone about this, do you understand?'

'Yes.'

'Go to mass now and recite the rosary with thankfulness for the preservation of your purity. Not a word to anyone!'

She hurried away to find Virginia. Just one more week to go before the election.

The young postulant who had been given such a fright, and such reliable guardian angels, no sooner agreed to comply with the strict commands of her immediate superior, than she felt free to talk about the great secret — which was already common knowledge. Perhaps she had blurted things out to someone in her first state of shock, in the corridor, or the kitchen where she had gone to fetch the morning bread? Or do walls have ears, mouths and voices? Anyway during that morning's lessons, and between the lessons, all the classes were astonished, asking questions, gossiping, exaggerating; boarders, day girls, nuns, priests.

'Well,' smiled Father Szelényi, his lips sucking his cigar like a baby its dummy, 'I rest content now. Nothing more can harm the Sisters of Mercy. If Beelzebub himself came disguised as a handsome prince, he would not defeat this convent. It has withstood the trial! If he wants to succeed he will have to come in the guise of a priest. Do you agree with me Sister Gregoria?'

They forgave his heavy irony. There was an underlying kindness and wisdom in his teasing tone of voice; and he was himself blameless.

'Erzsi, Erzsi,' Marika was running and panting, on good terms again with her older class mate. 'We could have great fun if you help me! You remember the report in the paper about that weird bet and how cross all the nuns were? We could make a sensational story of this for the Jewish paper. You are so good at it. They can't know about it yet; this lot are trying so hard to shush it up. They'll never know how the story got out. Isn't it a great idea?'

'No, no, no!' Erzsi was serious. 'The nuns would be most upset and it would do no good. We would have even more severe restrictions, a great inquisition, confessions, innocent suspects, we'd get no exeat for the rest of the year; poor Helen. . . . No. NO! Leave it alone.

We are here sharing their fare, which is good value even though we have to pay something for it.'

'Don't talk such trash! How boring you've got. I'll do it myself then and you can report me!'

'I'd never do that, you idiot!' answered Erzsi in a bad mood, shrugging her shoulders and walking on.

Next Sunday the new story did appear in the local paper. Marika's phrases were changed beyond recognition, all those flourishes she and Szidu had composed together on the dormitory floor — the report was more concise, but quite titillating enough. The naughty authors could be satisfied with the resulting small town tittle-tattle, and the angry dismay of the nuns. Berchtolda wrung her hands, Virginia was too dismayed to organize a grand inquisition. Simonea and the other retired nuns did not even bother to comment. They walked around silently condemning, in sorrowful superiority. They kept company with the nuns arriving from the outlying sister houses who filled up every vacant white-curtained cubicle, ready for the imminent election.

Before that *event,* the election, one of the younger Hungarian nuns left the convent; beautiful Gregoria spat blood and fell fainting in the staff room after her drawing lesson. Father Szelényi dropped his cigar on the floor and hurried over, he picked her up, carried her to the leather sofa. Huge beads of sweat fell from his forehead; he revived her, comforted her, like a father with his daughter — until the doctor arrived.

'We must get her away from here at once!' the doctor declared severely, having briefly examined her. 'How long have I been saying this? To the nursing home at Zólyom, if nowhere else is possible: another massive old convent building, thick stone walls, tiny windows, but anything is better than this place. And still teaching? Making her work in her condition. She wanted to?

Crazy — you are helping her to meet her maker; her heart is strong and she could have had many more years.'

This decent old convent doctor, a good Catholic man, was angry, and let fly about 'women folk without an Abbess' who make secret contracts with Death behind his back. He threatened to resign, was not going to give advice no one took, did not need this job, he would talk with the district inspector who was a good friend; this house was a nest of infection, 'a breeding place for germs' . . . and so on. . . . He took no notice, though they told him they had tried to give her rest periods for the last few months; but the sick woman had herself passionately wanted to teach and work at all cost, and would only get worse if forced to rest and if forbidden to go down to the room where all the convent accounts and business took place. He did not listen to their explanations.

Next day in the same office Virginia was feeling agitated during a conversation with their senior priest, Father Fénrich.

'May we please discuss some matters, Father? Now it's rather urgent. This is Wednesday, and on Sunday we have our election. We must request the Bishop, by letter, to appoint his representative — we would all like you to be in charge of the voting. Oh Heavens! We have had to ask Sister Evelina to take over from our poor dear Sister Gregoria and teach drawing. Nobody else is qualified. We ought to look through this document too, I am still not competent in legal matters. It's from Munich, from our postulant Helen Gross's guardian, a reply to a request (actually from the ward herself) that she should either cease to be considered a minor or that he should formally assign the gift of her worldly inheritance in favour of our Order, which will be her future home and family in Christ. Look what he writes

— he is not convinced by the religious vocation of his ward. It might merely be youthful whim (what a thing to say). He considers it his duty to take care of her fortune (how tiresome these Germans are, clinging to worldly goods, and I know for a fact he is a Protestant). In short, he wants time for Helen to consider her life, another six months. Has he the right to insist on this? Do the regulations of a German court still apply to our Helen? Oh dear, money! When will we be able to put our affairs in order? In four days it will be decided. We could have done without this wretched mendicant affair. If we only knew who told that wicked newspaper. (It's all starting up again; they have caught the criminals at Máramaros Island.) Let us hope they don't bring them here on charges of fraud, we don't want our people to be called as witnesses. Could you possibly deal with that? Perhaps a word to the Bishop's office. . . . Here are the plans for the enlargement of the garden building as a training institute. That has not been authorized yet — but we hope, with God's help, in four days time it will be. Father, you will dedicate today's mass for us as you promised, won't you? Oh my goodness . . . what is the matter. . . ? Are you ill? Oh dear Father?'

'Please leave me . . . for just a little while. . . . I can't concentrate on your affairs or those of the convent at the moment . . . I am so troubled.'

And he broke down crying on the desk.

'The threads of family ties are sometimes strong,' Virginia said gently looking on somewhat shocked, her face white and nervous. It was not seemly for her to suspect Father Fénrich in her thoughts. He was a consecrated priest.

The doctor's outburst on Gregoria's departure was also a topic for the nuns and the many visitors drifting in, day and night, from other convents. It was

Berchtolda's job to press for a new convalescent home in the mountains for nuns with TB; and for their old building to be upgraded at once to more modern standards of hygiene, for the whole community, not just one part or another. Money was needed for all these schemes; reliable new sources of finance, proper investment of their small capital, new schools, higher education, more internal members able to work; and to some extent an acceptance of the ways of the contemporary world — for example, electric lighting was permitted by the Church in some old buildings to replace traditional and expensive wax candles. Talking of electric light, how much quicker, safer, and more helpful it would have been in defending the community during that recent night attack — and generally how much better for the night watch to press a button for instant light, instead of a few flickering oil lamps beside the images along every corridor. How much cheaper it would be, how much easier, if there were telephone communications between different buildings! Many of the nuns enjoyed and approved such talk.

One evening (it was Friday, two days before the election), tactful Mother Simonea visited Berchtolda during *regracio*. She was extremely grave, a letter in her hand:

'Dear Sister, we have managed to intercept this disgraceful rubbish. The wicked authors are here within these holy walls, receiving the spiritual and material benefits of our Order; and I am shamed to say still wearing the postulant collar. Traitors! Imposters! Here among us, dear Sister, among the postulants under your supervision.'

'Oh what has happened now?' Berchtolda interrupted, frightened.

'Look at this and read it, dear Sister! This letter was

written by two of your pupils, the Kerekes sisters, to their accomplices, their parents who live in the town. It was hidden in the washerwoman's basket (our Domestic Sister has dismissed the woman, of course). She was apparently prepared to deliver it to her friend in town, the mother of those two. Read it!'

Berchtolda took the letter in her trembling hands and started to read where Simonea had marked it with her nail:

> Don't worry, dear Mum, we're alright. The food isn't as awful as you think; luckily it saves you all the worry of slaving away for our sakes. For sure, you would never have been able to pay for our tuition and lodging right up to the end of teacher training. And the clothes! With Dad always blaming you for everything when he's had too much to drink; we couldn't bear to see all that. So it has worked out quite well — getting all our training, board and lodging free here. After three years, on the very day we are through (they have to pass us as novitiates even if we never say a word during the teacher training course!) we'll come to you as two qualified teachers. Nothing can stop us! We won't have to give up our faith as we won't have taken final vows; and God will forgive us as our motive is filial love. They'll *have* to give us our diplomas or we'll take them to court; and we'll get jobs, then we can look after you. We'll do the work and earn enough for Dad to have his daily tobacco.
>
> Lots of love from your two ever loving and grateful daughters,
>
> Emma and Piroska.

'Oh, how often the evil spirit leads people into

temptation by exploiting their virtues!' Berchtolda was downcast. 'Their love for their mother was the cause.' She was inconsolable, had really liked the two Kerekes girls, calm and quiet, in their behaviour so natural. She had often held them up as examples of simple honesty.

'Tomorrow our time without a leader will end,' said Magdolna quietly when Virginia told her about this latest 'disgrace', the expulsion of the two Kerekes girls and the circumstances. 'I would like a firm strong hand again! I can hardly wait to call you Reverend Mother!'

'What . . . me? What are you saying?' Virginia looked shocked. (Was Magdolna really so unsuspecting? She was incapable of pretence.)

'Or will it be Berchtolda? I simply don't know who to vote for tomorrow. You only talk to me about great principles, with which, of course, I agree — but if anyone should ask me, I wouldn't know who should take responsibility for them. So tell me who shall I vote for?'

'Whoever you like, my dear!' Virginia answered, a little confused and with a reverence which always overcame her in the presence of this wonderful being. She could not explain but always felt Magdolna moved on a higher plane than the rest of them; and she believed she understood her qualities better, appreciated her more than any of the other nuns. This woman seemed pure, almost without sin, achieving this not by penitence, fasting or prayer, but simply by being from birth a good person, unable to be otherwise, and the Evil One had no power over her. Perhaps at some time, long ago — in the stormy outside world — she had overcome temptations. Or by study and reflection she had understood the secrets of the human soul — and body; so nothing was sinful in her, just as the doctor was innocent while touching and probing the chaste white breast of poor Gregoria. Oh, how Virginia longed for such a state of grace, to cast off burdens of doubt and worry. But then what would she do with her inexhaustible energy, with interests which were not sinful but a balance to other passions? Magdolna, her earthly exemplar, had lived and worked quietly among them, unaware of the dramas and intrigues around her. Virginia felt ashamed for all of them.

'Surely the individual does not matter so much?' continued the other musing on unfamiliar topics. 'We need a name, as a concept to which we can connect our notion of "obedience", which is simple and so wonderful for retaining our inner peace and freedom. I enjoy small restrictions and commands in daily observance and would not object to greater discipline. For the sake of inner freedom: it is good to know the boundaries, then there can be no trespass! During our interregnum we have had so many unpleasant distractions.'

'So you agree,' Virginia opened her eyes wide, 'with Leona's dictum that religious life can only be achieved with the old rigorous rules? That we *young ones* have "opened the gates to frivolity and unbridled licentiousness"?'

'Oh no — what are you saying, my dear? I would not blame anyone. I don't know all the circumstances as you do, and you must forgive me, but I have only just this minute thought about them. It has occurred to me . . . I shall feel a little sorry for whoever is elected tomorrow, she will carry such burdens and responsibilities as to lose the inner freedom of obedience.'

'She will have help in all the worries and the administration; she will bear responsibility for general principles,' Virginia urged feeling ever more depressed.

'Ah yes,' Magdolna smiled wearily, 'but while we others are freed from all those details of time, duties, travels, she has to accept responsibility on our behalf. What am I saying? Luckily, there are people with other gifts and temperaments, as for instance you, my dear! Please let me obey you; I shall only desire whatever you think is best. I can imagine no lighter or more pleasant task. I am most grateful to you.'

Virginia, sighing and confused, left her beloved friend to her prayers.

FOURTEEN

At last they sat crowded together, in the chapel which was freshly adorned with ivy, candles and incense. After mass they drifted towards the altar, knelt down in turn on the cold stone floor, necks slightly forward, parting their lips a little. The priest approached them one by one with the gold chalice and plate of the Holy Presence. Before their eyes he made the Sign of the Cross. In his hand appeared the deathly pallor of the Bridegroom's transparent body: the true Body and Blood in the mystery of the Host, every hour and every minute many thousands of times, perhaps to the end of time, taking the sins of the earth upon himself without torture or the shedding of blood; ever uniting in superhuman love, miraculously and totally with those who worship Him. They took care swallowing not to split that unity, the soul mingling in mythical union. Slowly, carefully they closed their mouths, not desecrating the Holy of Holies with their teeth; raised their eyes in ecstasy —

as if floating in wonder — closed them and rose in a daze to make room for others. They knelt once more on the first step, and whispering thanks, each struck her breast three times: 'Lord, I am not worthy to receive thee. . .'. Then they walked back, hands clasped, eyes half closed, slowly stepping on stone paving, holy purpose on their pale faces. They appeared relieved, harmonious and satisfied as after some great happy love. Back on their benches again they buried their faces in their hands to contemplate this greatest of miracles, the deepest and closest union with the Creator. The Lord of everything, dear Jesus of Nazareth whom they knew by name and could address familiarly — who for them, indeed for them, had spilled his blood on the cross. . . .

If the spirit had lost strength in constant repetition or through some present distraction, if they were unable to rekindle that happy awe which made the lives of saints blessed on this earth, they must not falter in performance; outward signs, forms, facial expression, must show reverence and avoid the risk of censure from other worshippers.

Father Fénrich, tired and in strange voice, after speaking a few words from the pulpit moved to the centre of the chapel where the urn was covered in a dark cloth. The chapel door was closed, voting began in secret. Throughout the convent — corridors, little chapels, cubicles, kitchens, laundry — there was not a single professed nun that morning, only pupils, postulants and novices. Geralda, in charge of the boarders, feverishly excited, commenced prayers from time to time. The hours passed and noon came slowly.

At half-past twelve they started to count the votes. Nuns in their benches were praying; Fénrich, Virginia and Simonea came to the end, looked at each other in disbelief. Dismayed they started counting again. In vain — the result was always the same. No result!

A little more than a third of the votes went to Leona, the rest were divided between Magdolna, Simonea and Virginia. Three votes were cast for that self-denying saint Evelina. So there it was! After so much correspondence, canvassing, organizing of cliques. Unpleasant events of the last weeks had upset the mood and clouded the issues; smaller parties were formed, each had her own opinion. This was the result: 'We have no Mother!' Simonea and Virginia spoke almost together in despair. Father Fénrich pronounced that His Grace the Bishop would declare another day for election, as there was no clear majority for any candidate: the two who had received most votes, Leona and Magdolna, would go forward for the next election. It was clearly stated in the Order's letter of foundation, that a new Reverend Mother must have a two-thirds majority of the total electorate. As His Grace was now on a pastoral journey, they must perforce await his return, and nuns from the sister houses would not be able to depart before that time.

They proceeded to the dining room, heads cast down, unable to give glad tidings to the throng of novices waiting at the chapel door. They could not have their modest feast of celebration in the decorated dining room; they put aside for a more suitable occasion the cold dishes, the cake and the careful ration of half a glass of wine per person; the dispirited flock without a shepherdess dished out their soup in silence. The most depressed countenance of all was Magdolna's; Virginia's heart contracted with fright when she stole glances at her. She had to ask if they could talk after the meal. They hurried along the corridors, stepped into an empty classroom and stopped face to face on the low platform as upon a stage; Magdolna's face was dark, her voice unusually strict:

'Tell me why. Why did you do this to me?'

'Magdolna, Magdolna, I honour you so much, you must know that! I cannot consider anyone more special than you, of higher worth; no one more worthy of ruling over us.'

'More worthy? And how about *suitable*, Sister Virginia?'

'Oh please don't look at me like that, don't speak to me so sternly! I couldn't know, how . . . how much this disturbs you.'

'Do you not know me? How can you say you love me?'

'No, never . . . never doubt that!' Virginia cried out in passion. 'I am so depressed by everything, everything has gone so wrong. God's Judgement. Oh, it could be that my love for you is not right, Magdolna. Perhaps it is sinful, please tell me, judge me, you understand everything. You know you are everything for me, my love of life, my hope, my purpose. I only wanted it for you, to please you. I can only enjoy my work through you, all the earthly struggles. Only through you can anything really hurt me, even — my sins — Oh God help me! I have never loved a fellow human so much; maybe it is impossible for anyone to do so.'

'Sister Virginia! What are you saying my friend! Pull yourself together!'

'No, no I can't be sensible anymore. I've agonized so much, and my feelings are ever more powerful. It's not a childish thing . . . as is common here in the convent. It rules my whole soul, all my better feelings, all my thoughts. Oh God, I've made my confession! Give me your hand, Magdolna, my Magdolna — please touch my forehead.'

'Sister Virginia!' Magdolna shouted to rouse her and stepped aside to hide her horror and distaste. 'Virginia get up at once. What can you mean by kneeling in front of a fellow human being, what would anyone who might walk in here think?'

'What? It would be best to die now.'

She stood there, face drawn, habit disordered, veil crumpled — shame and distress in her eyes; half aware that her idiotic passions had been rejected. Her nervous mouth twitched, all of her face trembled; her mouth was so dry she could hardly utter any words. . . . Magdolna seeing suffering and humiliation returned to her customary gentle self, all anger evaporating. She held out a soothing hand.

'Sister Virginia, calm down — come,' she said kindly and led Virginia to the podium chair by the large table (they were in the fourth-year classroom). 'Let's talk things over,' she continued smiling a little, 'you are overwrought and that is not surprising, you have worked so hard for the community. My dear Virginia, you must not think I judge you, or misunderstand you, though I can't fall in with you. It was wrong of me to speak harshly a moment ago. We have such different personalities, different backgrounds, different physical needs. You imagined me in your own image, proposed for me what you would have chosen for yourself — to carry the burden of leadership here. *Not yet* perhaps but later when you are older, surely. And this other . . . this other . . . your nervousness, I do believe is a little illness or a special condition; it is in proper circumstances, and in some places, natural — there is such variety in life and in people and in emotions, Virginia, and everything human can be true and wonderful. So I have read, and I only know from hearsay; but it is in the nature of this world that we never fully understand each other. We must strive to love each other in the right way. Listen to me, and I'll tell you what I think about it.'

Holding her hand, Magdolna talked to Virginia quietly, sensitively, for a long time — until Virginia's trembling ceased and she raised her head more confidently. Early spring dusk had fallen, scented evening breezes wafted between them from the open first-floor window. They parted with a warm sisterly handshake. This fourth-form classroom was to remain in the memory of one of these nuns forever. The deepest, most dramatic scene of her life had taken place there, her greatest suffering and also a healing calm. She hurried to the silent chapel still numb in feeling and movement — but with an understanding of emotions she had hitherto feared, or fought in blind uncertainty. She was confident now that her own 'deep' feelings were no different from the pupils' foolish yearning and sighs, or Kunigunda's clumsy sentimentality, though it had seemed more spiritual and serious: no more natural or holy for her than for the others, but caused by an environment which could lead one astray. She also understood that the same human destiny led her as led Father Fénrich and poor Sister Gregoria, and just how harshly she had judged it. How wonderful to discover understanding for others, the whole race! She remembered her mother marrying the handsome fencing master so soon after becoming a widow and understood now the root of her own violent hatred towards him. All these things were connected. That ancient true instinct was given by God himself in Paradise, and He had sanctified this oldest sacrament as marriage. Nuns, specially chosen by God, made vows of chastity for all their lives, to serve a firmer purpose than ordinary duty, reach higher perfection by keeping the commandments. How lucky at last to understand herself and others; the laws of nature, animals, trees; the inter-connections of knowledge, and the function of human organs. She was filled with gratitude for Magdolna who had so lucidly, simply explained all this to her. She had to get to thirty-five before the facts of life were clear to her; but felt she would be a better person and a better nun from that moment on. She knelt before the altar, hands lightly clasped, looking ahead with calm open eyes, absorbed in deep prayer.

The Bishop was not due back for another week and until then all the visiting nuns, hardly squeezing into the place, were to pass the time idly. Meanwhile, in the sister houses there would be no work, no teaching, no domestic supervision; in hospitals throughout the country the sick would wait in vain for experienced nurses. What a mess . . . what an 'unausstehliche muddle' — Kunigunda croaked around each day, grumbling, with her bloated face. The visitors themselves were uneasy, like mothers of families who very seldom leave home: what disasters might be happening without them? They had not brought linen or underwear for such a long stay. A few novices from the distant sister houses sent parcels for their Reverend Mothers, others received requests by letter or telegram. There was constant coming and going by the porta; messengers, traders and cleaning women handed the bell pull over from one to another.

FIFTEEN

In all this confusion, at dusk (which Erzsi had anxiously awaited), they managed it without mishap. Helen Gross wore the shapeless hat and short coat that belonged to the day girl who lodged with Mrs Fóth. Erzsi contrived a complete day-girl uniform — shabby grey skirt, gloves and all — receiving them clandestinely beneath a desk in the new building during a teaching method lesson. She had smuggled them along corridors to the main building in constant dread of Kunigunda and others of the old gang. In one of the cubicles Erzsi helped the postulant to put on her disguise, carefully hid the abigail collar under that strange coat, and ruffled Helen's hair to make it look worldly enough for the hat. She hurried her down the back stairs (some special deity protecting them), mingled for a minute with the throng at the gate, and at a suitable moment, when the door was open for others to pass through, gave a strong shove to Helen's arm and whispered, 'Now!' Erzsi could only glance for a second, enough to observe the shy girl entranced by the daylight at the gateway, by the wonderful sounds of an outside world . . . street noises, the scent of fresh leaves and dust, a sense of free and happy women out for their evening stroll. One moment — then the gate was shut, the corridor dark until the next bell.

Erzsi tiptoed upstairs, and sighed with relief. She almost breathed a prayer of gratitude for the success of her dangerous mission. What had she done? She had helped a postulant to escape; she had let fifty thousand koronas escape. If it had been possible, Helen could have left the new building by the cattle gate, together with the day girls — but she had not been allowed down to attend teacher training courses for some time. They were forced into greater deception. Along dormitory corridors in daylight with a girl dressed in street clothes. They had encountered so many people on the ground floor, and all those nuns, and nobody had stopped them or asked why they were there. At no other time would this have happened, only in this present chaos. . . . 'Gelobt sei Jesus Christus', said Erzsi; it was old Simonea, she had nodded 'In Ewigkeit', without a word of query to them. . . . Now here on this corridor, she could tell any tale she liked. But she still had to get to the parlour without a mishap; she could hear the voice of the Old One. Gidu was stepping out of a room, holding her music books.

'Give me your key; quick, you are going to practise anyway. It must look as if I'm coming out of here!'

'Where have you been?'

'Shush.' Holding the key in her hand she walked nonchalantly in front of the Old One's desk; Kunigunda was giving Janka Militorisz a thorough scolding for some 'trespass'.

An hour later, just before supper, a postulant came

to ask whether anyone had seen 'our dear candidate' Helen Gross? Might she have come here for some reason, been taken ill, some other trouble? The Old One happened to be in a good mood; gave Berchtolda's messenger a piece of her mind about untidy, undisciplined, unruly novices, who have to be chivvied every evening like geese to their nests. If only she were in charge she would show them! Then Berchtolda herself came in almost running, indignation bursting from her face, a piece of paper in her hand. Even the Old One was upset by her story, and showed some sympathy. Her indignant denial, 'No one from here. *No, no!*', was heard quite clearly by Szidu. 'You don't need help from anyone to escape from this present chaos! No, dear Sister, *my* girls don't wander harum-scarum about the house, that's not my kind of discipline!'

Berchtolda, quite cast down, hurried away. At supper Gidu was able to bring all the news to the boarders. Her informant was a novice in the music room, her friend, Emerika. According to her (Erzsi knew it all, of course, as she'd cooked it up), Berchtolda had received an apologetic letter, signed *your grateful admirer, Helen Gross,* in which the young postulant respectfully informed her that she was no longer a postulant and had departed from the convent in the early hours of the afternoon; she would be living for the next few weeks with her kind Catholic friend, Mrs Holzer, in the town (with the permission of her guardian), until her marriage to Albert Toffler, a teacher. She had received so much kindness in the convent and now asked forgiveness for her sudden departure without any goodbyes or explanations; she had been anxious to avoid explanations and possible recriminations, and so on. Erzsi listened to this précis of her composition and wondered whether, before seeing her fiancé, simple Helen might have changed out of her ugly clothes into some smart blouse of Mrs Holzer's? Surely she would not turn up in that awful abigail collar to meet her intended?

The time for Erzsi to feel anxious — and she hadn't prepared herself — had only just begun, as the investigations got under way to discover who might have helped plot this terrible disaster, depriving the precious convent of so much money. The inquisition was conducted with less severity than had been customary for smaller offences than this. Virginia, usually the passionate organizer of such matters, was (strangely) lukewarm on this occasion. Berchtolda felt very guilty, and feared recriminations, considering herself responsible for influencing this unworthy perverse person; Simonea and her friends felt the same — worried in retrospect about their perhaps dubious role. They all agreed 'we nurtured a viper in our bosom'. It was impossible for them to act against this carefully planned deceit, and the inevitable had to be accepted: they vilified 'the little cheat', 'slow waters run deep', 'that decadent flirt of a city girl', 'well, good luck to her husband!' And the young nuns were most indignant of all.

'No good will come from that type of street girl. If she can deceive Our Lord in that way how much more will she cheat other people? She will always be a slut!' Geralda gave her opinion to the boarders, talking to them from beside Helen's old bed; anybody could tell she came from Budapest, by these occasional lapses into city slang.

The more senior ones continued their lament on behalf of the late Reverend Mother (poor soul); it would have killed her; lucky she had died before it all happened! Sister Adele, in charge of the nursery, only mentioned the affair once when she angrily declared:

'Foolish girl! She thinks it's worthwhile for a man —

doesn't she realize they are all the same: deceivers, wicked, cunning!'

Only gradually, a few of them dared to suggest that marriage was also a sacrament decreed by God in Paradise.

All the visitors from other places had plenty to discuss and talk about during that week; nuns from the convent, the elderly and middle-aged who had formed two opposing factions, drew closer together in righteous indignation. Both parties ignored the main ground of their anger: money, the German girl's dowry. Now they could neither afford a new teaching block, nor a sanatorium for TB patients. Nor could they solve their immediate financial troubles or carry on just as they were before. That little sum, fifty thousand koronas, had escaped from under their noses — old and young were equally aware of it. But no one mentioned it at all, not liking to call a spade a spade.

One feeling was paramount and urgent: these terrible days must end — by whatever means. Everyone could then carry on with her work, say daily prayers and have no further worries. Many of them were saying that all the organizing, canvassing and bureaucratic fuss was 'not suitable for our Order'. Others felt more strongly:

'Who should we choose? We did not join to *choose* — we joined to *obey*! It does not matter who it will be. Our days are spent in the valley of tears, soon the hour of death will be upon us, as we recall fifty-three times at each telling of the rosary. Our span on earth is short, not worth too much fuss.'

This was the latest mood throughout the overcrowded old house and its wings; boarders in their day room were the exception. Quite different topics absorbed them; they were eager for news, thrilled for the *happy bride*. Mrs Fóth's lodger brought information every day to Erzsi and on to the rest of them. They discussed the messages Helen sent: Toffler was such a dear man; they would soon exchange rings for the official betrothal; Mrs Holzer was so kind and very much hoped they would all be equally happy one day.

'Foul weather for a betrothal,' muttered Kunigunda on the day, with a mixture of anger, jealousy, gentleness and curiosity, as she watered her pot palm in the parlour and looked out to the overcast spring sky.

Behind her young Geralda repeated:

'She is just a common slut!'

Senior girls hid behind their text books. . . . May the young couple out there be blessed with sunshine from behind that thin veil of cloud.

One evening, at the end of the week, with the Bishop's return expected, old Simonea called on Berchtolda during *regracio*. The visitor was at her most charming, and the hostess smiling, considerate; they had greeted each other in the corridors recently with deep courtesy. One could sense these new moods — a release of tension was usually mutual, and had some hidden meaning.

'I have come to you, dear Sister,' Simonea started; 'Sister Virginia is so depressed, or has seemed so for the past days; perhaps as last year, she is not quite well. But she is strong and will pull herself together — the best remedy is a hair shirt and fasting as St Vincent taught us. I would like to talk a little with you concerning our beloved convent and the affairs of our Order, which seem to be in trouble. Could we talk together? I would so much value your advice about turning this danger and decadence to good use.'

'Oh, that is my greatest wish too!' answered the Mistress of the Novitiate. 'If only I knew what I, lowest of God's servants, could do in this terrible situation. Believe me, dear Sister, I — all of us are ready for anything. . . .'

'God will aid us, dear Sister, I can say that with certainty. Throughout my life I have experienced the Love of God and his special care for us, His nuns. We must have Faith. Magdolna, our Sister, devout and blessed with special gifts, has been to see me today and most sincerely explained her unsuitability, by reason of her temperament, for the duties of a Reverend Mother. She assured me, as I had suspected, her name had been put forward without her knowledge or consent. God has not called her to our Order for that purpose, but to enhance the quality of our schools. She will be needed even more in the future, when we open the Higher Training College as planned by you and the other younger nuns; we older nuns, who once opposed this, now fully recognize the need.'

Berchtolda could only nod in silent astonishment.

'She also humbly asked to be allowed to return to the sister house for a few years, and has important reasons for this transfer; she will ask permission as soon as possible from our new Head. Perhaps she is overscrupulous, fearing that her presence here after this election, might disturb the next Reverend Mother. These factions are quite unworthy of our Order, we are all guilty, and it will be best when we put such matters behind us. Should Magdolna depart to our large community beyond the Danube, where dear Sister Virginia was planning to open a senior college, perhaps she could take the position of local principal?'

Again Berchtolda nodded.

'As for a girls' secondary school . . . Sister Berchtolda, we might perhaps pause a little before that project. Why should we, in our poverty, pioneer this so publicly? We don't as yet have enough suitable people. We need you here where you are. Virginia will surely work with the new Reverend Mother, as before; she will be more needed than ever. If our respected Sister Leona is elected unanimously — as is seemly — she would concentrate upon a saintly life and the practice of spiritual virtue, for her body is frail and elderly. We would need the help of Sister Virginia who, as secretary to our late Mother, achieved such distinction for us through her qualities of dedication and competence. Let's for the moment forgo the secondary school and other premature schemes — would you agree? Really how could anyone, with genuine love for our Order, rigidly oppose some renovation of our house; or certain improvements learnt from the outside world! I am confident our clever Virginia will find a way despite the present financial restraints. Regarding the sanatorium, which has been proposed for such a long time, I myself have a modest suggestion. Our old house at Zólyom may not be suitable but I do know that pleasant and inexpensive houses are being built there. I have already mentioned this to our doctor and he agrees that they would be fine — if we can find a simple place not too near any neighbours.'

'Dear Sister,' sighed Berchtolda, 'what trouble might be avoided if we could always speak so frankly together in mutual trust!'

'We are all of us guilty, my dear; but it is never too late to acknowledge and learn from our mistakes. We — you know — are old, tired out by work; we shall soon face the final judgement. Sister Leona is one of the old nun's dearest friends, from before the time we entered the Order. Long ago as young girls we travelled here together, to a foreign land, to follow our Redeemer. Gentle Sister, that journey! The farewells (we knew it was forever) from our parents and relatives, our native land; we were only sixteen years old.

Mostly we travelled by the old coaches, sometimes on farm wagons, sometimes on foot. . . . "German whores! Foreign trash!" the peasants shouted at us — I should call them villagers. Now I understand what those words meant. Our long departed first Reverend Mother, Leona's sister, was just twenty years old at that time, senior to all of us. The two sisters came from my village, daughters of a wealthy butcher; they left family and worldly wealth to follow Jesus. Oh, how many have now gone to join Him, in the eternal bliss of Heaven! Dear Sister Berchtolda, you must forgive us old nuns this whim: for our Reverend Mother we would like to have the sister of our first Mother. She is a kind of founder of this house with us . . . it will be yours in effect, my dear, we know that well; and how many useful, true tasks you will perform while we only have whims — and memories; perhaps you will allow us those!'

Berchtolda took out her large handkerchief to wipe incipient tears.

'I have gossiped too long tonight about my generation and myself, please forgive me for taking up precious time. I did want to mention a few more details on which I'd like your agreement — but I have almost finished. Oh yes, one more thing! On no account would we wish to entrust the novices to anyone else's care. With your maternal sense and wonderful tact you have done a marvellous job. Three times as many girls have felt vocations since you took over — more in one year than the whole number of novices we usually have at any one time. This is a great service to our Order; we need more nuns, we can manage then with fewer paid lay sisters. We have gathered such a large young flock, we must do all we can to train them in the true spirit. We shall have to examine them strictly lest we nurture among them such deceitful spirits as those two Kerekes sisters, whose name I do not even like to mention. To make your burden lighter, and to offer the young girls a very high example, we thought it would be helpful to give you as an assistant in your work, our most saintly nun, Sister Evelina.'

'My duty will be submission to the new Reverend Mother's commands,' answered Berchtolda, her face slightly clouded. She accepted the final bitter pill: to have as her controller that self-denying, silent, gloomy, eyes-cast-down saint. Nothing mattered now, or so she thought at that moment.

This long friendly conversation had one result. No further election was necessary. A memorandum sent to his Grace the Bishop, signed by all the professed nuns, asked him to appoint Sister Leona as Reverend Mother.

SIXTEEN

Happy month of May! Love, innocence, happiness, young couples; month of Mary and of blossom; month of the Blessed Virgin, Bride of God.

A painting of the Virgin as expectant mother — among Murillo clouds and roses — was on the main altar of their chapel. Angel faces crowded around, roses flushed with red appeared from the curtain of clouds, little cupids, pagan putti. From her head radiated a garland of stars; beneath her feet the orb of the full moon, she floated in triumph above the Serpent's head. Persephone in spring triumphing over the Darkness of secret, sick, winter moods . . . blessed mystery; transparent veil; youth!

How lovely to sit in calm oblivion within that chapel for long hours of the afternoon, aware of the incense and the scent of flowers, hearing again the words of that simple and haunting ancient story; responding as a congregation in quiet rhythm: 'Gate of Heaven . . .

Guardian of Holy Matrimony . . . Tower of Ivory . . . Rose of Mystery!'

Secular brides from the town, young betrothed couples, enjoyed celebrating with song the rites of spring in this flowery chapel; the special litany of Mary in this convent. Boarders could glimpse bare-headed men strangely clothed in the courtyard. One Sunday there appeared through the light of the archway a handsome young couple arm in arm. The fiancée wore a beautiful white dress and hat trimmed with flowers; her alert face still showed traces of spots; dreamily she gazed into the gloom of the convent corridors. As she caught sight of Erzsi she gave a naughty smile and nudged her young man's arm to draw his attention. He took off his hat and smiled gratefully to the stranger, their kind fairy.

'Hurr-rry upp! Disgraceful!', the Old One shouted at the first pair of girls.

'Did you see Helen?' 'Helen Gross?' 'Our old Helen!' The whispers buzzed round the line of boarders.

'QUI-ETT! Brazen hussies!' Kunigunda was yelling at them, and overturned the teatime bread basket in her anger.

The young betrothed couple came next day and the following days; no one could forbid them to attend chapel.

'Her heart draws her back to us, after all,' said one of the nuns who had been fond of Helen, and honoured the memory of the previous Reverend Mother. 'Her eyes are so like her aunt's, don't you think?'

Sometimes Helen would shyly greet them: 'Gelobt sei. . . !' They responded; it would have been wrong not to do so.

One day Virginia happened to pass the young couple in the courtyard; she stopped unexpectedly, looked deep into the girl's eyes. Helen bent down and kissed the nun's hands fervently.

'Are you happy?' asked the nun seriously.

'Oh yes, dear Sister, truly happy. May I present my fiancé to you: he is such a devout Catholic. Dear kind Sister!'

Almost in tears she again bent to kiss Virginia's hand. This was graciously permitted in holy fashion.

'I will pray for you, my child. Our dear lately departed is surely praying for you above. She was so wise and good.'

'Dear Sister, would you allow me, would the convent receive a gift from me? I would like to present a new altar cloth of fine material with real gold and silver embroidery, and the robes to go with it — I would be so very happy!'

'I will try and see to it my child,' answered Virginia and brushed the bride's cheek in an episcopal gesture. She reflected it would be unwise to antagonize a rich Catholic woman.

Calculating again, organizing, planning; just as before. Could she have done otherwise? It was her nature.

The boarders had heard already, via Marika the know-all, that Magdolna would not be teaching there next year, saintly Evelina was appointed as an example to Berchtolda's novices, and Virginia would continue to be secretary of everything by the side of the new Reverend Mother. Fundamentally, nothing had changed — or very little! Only what absolutely had to change; brought about by the passage of time in its own slow rhythm. Things cannot be hurried, forced, but neither can they be held back and avoided. Life goes its own way; and of the things we would like to happen, prescribe with our own will power, perhaps only a fraction can ever be achieved. This might be considered disheartening, or the happy medium way known as compromise. But that's how things happen in the outside world; and should happen even more so in a convent. *It is of no importance*. People entered to spend their lives, because this life does not matter. Our days are numbered in the valley of tears, will quickly pass, until the final reckoning comes; the only important event, of which we are reminded fifty-three times at each telling of the rosary: 'Now and in the hour of our death'.

The pupils and senior boarders no longer puzzled themselves about such philosophical convent themes. They were gravitating outwards; would leave soon and enter the fresh air. Others would take their place, by which time the bright young green leaves of the trees would be falling, the tension of imagined worries diffusing into the open healthy corridors. Father Szelényi smiling, strolled among them frightening the girls with his tales of the viva examinations: the terrible consequences if any cribbing were to be discovered, if any bits of paper microscopically written were found among the ample shawls of the novices or in coils of the day girls' hair.

Fourth-year girls spent their days in the leafy garden, preparing for their finals from morning till night. Without Kunigunda, without supervision, eight or ten of them could wander along the wide paths under those great trees, with the petals falling, new buds swelling on the lilac bushes, breathing the dank spring smell of shrub roots; the bright green lawn grass, the blue of the sky, nests, soft breezes, feathers, dreams, clouds, eternal hymn to the month of May. Youth. . . .

Everything, always, beginning anew.

Father Szelényi holding his cigar strolled among the tender cabbage shoots, beyond the wire fence of their garden. Szidu and Gidu and a few others crowded round him. He had to be coaxed when they wanted him to talk but once started he was away on some theme no matter what it happened to be:

'My dear girls, in the study of Science it is not a question of Truth — that does not exist, apart from Religion. God in his benevolence has given us our Faith. Science is concerned with *connections*, that is the point; new and productive ideas which connect very easily and simply with other ideas. Do you follow me? I wonder if you do. The concept of "conjecture" does not occur in scientific "truth", only in fairy tales: wouldn't you agree? Why the devil should it exist; what use would it be to you or me? Someone has written about this as a speculation, and so it will remain among scientists for just as long as they can explain phenomena more simply in their own way. Once we get beyond, then "conjecture" can be pensioned off, it will have answered a need. Why did I say *more simply*, Miss Gizella? Never mind, don't worry your little head. It's perfectly possible to explain the movements of the sun and moon and the whole solar system by ancient geocentric theories; of course, it's more clumsy, takes longer and there are more gaps. By putting the sun in the centre, it is easier, fewer problems, simpler — so that's why the sun is in the centre, for simplicity, my dears. By the time the pigment in Miss Szidu's hair fades to grey, I suspect the theory of "ethereal tremors" (which you forgot in the last lesson and therefore got low marks), will suffer the same sad fate and be itself forgotten. Because recently some mischievous fellows have begun to discover "an-ti-pa-the-tic" matter, which little by little erodes the earlier much respected theory. For decades it has prospered and brought cheap lighting to an ungrateful humanity. A few more such impertinent discoveries and a brave fellow will come along to hit it on the head: bang!

An end to ethereal trembling! There will be other "sacred truths", new ones — or very possibly the return of some old theories: like that of moonshine containing magic potions for lovers' dreams. . . . What do you all think?'

They said nothing; only smiled, they were young. While the old man talked light rain had begun to fall, and he opened his large umbrella. Still the girls did not move. They seemed unaware of occasional drops of water on their heads, or that it was getting thicker and heavier; they continued to stand together, motionless around the old sage of the garden, eyes fixed on him. They barely heard what he said (he did not expect them to), they were so fond of his fat face, his pleasure in his own risqué wit, they did not want to appear as 'silly girls'; a little rain could not deter them from a science lecture.

The sun came out again; opposite the cabbage beds, among newly weeded tomato plants, the elegant girlish figure of Cornelia Popescu could be seen. She was walking by the side of Father Kapossy, each of them holding a text book. Were they discussing some academic questions before the exam? Impossible to tell; certainly both had such serious expressions on their faces, the most cynical of nuns or even saintly Evelina herself could not have found fault with them. At this time sad farewells were in the air.

Erzsi Király was looking out from among the leaves, careful of any lurking danger; reassured she darted from the lilac bushes to the further fence. She knew that long suburban gardens stretched out on the other side and one in particular belonged to the parents of a day-girl friend. Fani Grünberger would be walking and studying just there — mugging up her lessons aloud, cheeks sunken and her face tired from so much effort: Fani was an excellent student. She had a friend with her, Erzsi's messenger from the town who brought in love letters and sometimes received truffles sent mysteriously from Budapest.

'Erzsi! Yes! I have been hiding a letter in my text book for the last three days.'

'Thank you, my dear! Slip it into my geology book. There is no one here but it is best to take care. Where have you got to? Finished the Middle Ages? What about physics? . . . Terrible, like a mill grinding away. We are still at the Punic Wars, and spectra analysis. Who do you think will get distinctions? Of course you will, Fani.'

'Certainly not me. A Jewish girl!' Fani flushed with pleasure.

'Oh, the nuns aren't like *that*. They'll give it to you just to show how broad-minded they are with other religions. Let's bet on it.'

'I bet they won't give me a distinction!' Fani shouted almost trembling with agitation.

'What shall it be? A box of chocolates? Done. My dear, do me a favour, get in touch with your dress-maker friend — because, you know, I have to have my new dress and travelling cape ready for the final *Te Deum*. Very important.'

'Heavens! Are you going far away?'

'Up to Budapest.'

'As far as that? What will you do there?'

'Nothing. Look around the city for a while.'

'Lucky thing!' the two young scholars exclaimed almost together — surprised, suspicious, jealous. They fell silent. Bees buzzed on the spring bushes, lilac buds were breaking into colour, occasionally brushing gently against their young faces.